Utopia Realized:

In Search of a Just Society

Utopia Realized:

In Search of a Just Society

Kurt Warner

This edition published in 2025
by Maida Vale Publishing
an imprint of Eyewear Publishing Ltd,
The Black Spring Press Group
London, United Kingdom

Cover design by Juan Padron
Typeset by Subash Raghu

ISBN 978-1-915406-45-3

www.blackspringpressgroup.com

To my wonderful Mother, who showed me what utopia really means.

"Pauperism must go. But industrialism is no remedy... [The evil] lies in our selfishness and want of consideration for our neighbors."

"Industrialism is, I am afraid going to be a curse for mankind. Exploitation of one nation by another cannot go on for all time. Industrialism depends entirely on your capacity to exploit..."

"Replace greed by love and everything will come right."
– 'Village Development and Economy of Country', and *Young India*, M.K. Gandhi

"The call is for service, and, such is the wholesomeness of it, he who serves all, best serves himself."
– Introduction to Upton Sinclair's 1915 *Anthology of Justice*, Jack London

"Do to others as you would have them do to you."
– Holy Bible, New International Version, Matthew 7:12, Luke 6:31

CONTENTS

PROLOGUE

"I can't just work harder all the time, Kristen!" John Matthews said sternly as he squeezed the steering wheel in anger and frustration. Thick and large beads of sweat accumulated not only on his forehead but on the steering wheel due to his hands. His eyes were bloodshot, and his thick, black hair was uncombed. He spoke into his cell phone which he held to his ear as he drove to work.

"Yes, I'm always hearing about what you can't do, John, but what can you do to help us get out of this hole? We're two months late on the rent, and the eviction notice we just received gives us ten days to figure it out. What, exactly, do you suggest we should do?"

John shook his head and tried to focus on the highway. He was driving to work and the drive, with traffic, typically took twenty minutes. John and Kristen had found an apartment that was markedly cheaper just outside of the center city of Scranton and the savings on the rent made it worth the commute.

"I don't know, Kristen. What I do know is that one way or another, I'll figure it out. How many notices to quit have we received in the past?"

"Too many! It's been four, at this point, and I don't see any end in sight to the nightmare that is living here."

"But how many times have we gotten kicked out, honey?"

"We haven't."

"Exactly. I always found a way to make it work, and I will find a way to make it work this time. You already know that I picked up the second job as a cashier at Sheetz, and between the income of that, your income, and mine, we should be able to meet all our financial obligations this month. I will figure out a way to work out the rest with Stanley when I talk to him. Whenever I'm actually able to sit down and look him in the eye, he's been willing to give me a little bit more time. He's a reasonable man. He's got a two-year-old too and that makes him understand what it's like, you know? His understanding is what has gotten us the last four extensions, and we'll get this one too."

"Well, I'm glad at least one of us is confident."

John smiled sheepishly, and his exhausted eyes continued to look heavy with yesterday's fatigue.

"I'm not confident, honey. But I am determined. I know that I can get us, one way or another, through the next day. What I'm having trouble with is looking farther down the road. When I do that, I don't see any end in sight. That's what brings fear and trembling into me. How can we create the life we want when no matter what we do, we're in a hole? If it's not due to the landlord, then it's the car company, the insurance company, the electric company… the list never ends!"

As John finished, he continued holding his cell phone to his ear. He was now driving on Highway 712, the road which leads to Scranton High School. John's shift as the janitor there began each day at seven in the morning and he was used to the morning rides to work. The traffic in Scranton was never too congested because it is not a large enough city for it to be overwhelming. However, there are two general times when the traffic is significant. One was in the morning and the other was in the evening. John drove steadily at around fifty-five miles per hour as he drove the two-lane highway.

Both sides of the highway had a slight ravine on either side. The Pennsylvania Department of Transportation designed this to create a way for rainwater, snow, and other debris to be deposited into the ravine rather than remain on the road.

John looked around at the landscape of the city in which he lived and worked as he drove to his job. The city was built in the middle of the Moosic Mountains, which surrounded it on all sides. John admired them and especially admired the way they formed a structure around the city and seemed to hug and protect it from the world.

John enjoyed history a great deal and read whenever he had time. He often imagined these large and majestic mountains as a natural version of the Colosseum and the town of Scranton as the arena where the battles were fought. On his tired and exhausted drives into work, he thought of himself as a gladiator in this arena. He saw his every day as a way of fighting for his livelihood in much the same way that some of those brave and tortured souls had to fight back in those most ancient of days. The scenery around him always evoked these thoughts and the commute painfully and regrettably prepared him for the daily battle he felt he was about to fight. For John, it was a man-made pit in which so many human beings toiled and suffered.

The sun pierced through the trees and was overwhelmingly bright and beautiful on its ascent into the Scranton sky that autumn morning. That morning, it shone so brightly and rose so quickly that everyone driving into and out of Scranton had their visor down as they focused on their drive.

However, on this specific day, John did not focus on the mountains, scenery, or his daily battle. Instead, he was filled with other anxieties, and that angst, combined with his lack of sleep, consumed all of his conscious thought.

"You know that's not our only problem, John. Isabella doesn't have enough formula and we've used up all the food stamps and the charities around here only let us go once a month."

John shook his head and gripped the steering wheel harder. "I know, honey. I know we don't have enough for her and it kills me every day. Why do you think I keep pushing so hard? That little girl means everything to me."

"I know she does, John. But her meaning everything to you does not get us what we need. Your job doesn't get us what we need. Your second job doesn't get us what we need. My work doesn't get us what we need. I mean, what are we going to do?"

John glanced at the hairline crack in his windshield that he was never able to get fixed. His eyes looked over at the seat next to him. He saw the tear in the seat and the fabric that continued to come out of it. He heard the rough running of the engine and knew about the head gasket leak that caused the reverberating sound that he heard constantly. He could smell the odor of burnt oil at every moment and knew he had other leaks, too that needed to be repaired. He knew each of these issues would compound his problem in time but he could not afford to pay attention to them now.

"I don't know what else to do but keep working as hard as I can, Kristen. With my two jobs, along with you working as hard as you can, I feel we just got to hope it all works out."

"Rather than just hoping it all works out, why don't you try again to get a teaching position at the school or an administrative position of some kind?"

"Teaching position? I could apply if you want me to, but I don't see much use in it. If I apply for anything like that, I'm going to get rejected on the basis of my not having the right qualifications."

"Well, you don't know unless you try. Who knows? Maybe one of them will take pity on you."

John felt irritated. "Kristen, what is the point of me applying for something that I will not get? Doesn't that seem a little irrational to you? Does it seem like I have a lot of free time between my two jobs, my wife and my child, to be running around filling out applications for jobs I have no shot at obtaining? Even if the school did want to hire me as a history teacher or as an administrator, I would never be able to be hired because the state sets the qualifications, and I just don't meet any with my GED."

"Well, what would you need, John?"

"I'd say an associate's degree at the least, and almost definitely a bachelor's degree for most teaching jobs. Ron, Melissa, Susan, and Michelle all have bachelor's degrees, and they are all teachers here."

Kristen paused a few moments and then cleared her throat. She said, "So then, go and get your bachelor's degree. You'd be an amazing history teacher. And if that would get us out of the red, why not?"

John continued to hold his phone up to his ear as he spoke and navigated the highway with his right hand on the wheel.

'Well, let's play that out. Let's just say I started going to the community college to get my associate's. That would take up at least enough of my time for me to have to quit my new job at Sheetz, if not have to quit my janitor job. How quickly do you think we'll get evicted, then? How much food, clothes and medical bills would we be able to afford for ourselves and our beautiful daughter if I did that?"

Kristen became very quiet on the other end of the phone. After a while, she stated, "It's the same thing if I went to school. There's no way out, is there? There's no next move on the chessboard, is there? We will never have healthcare. We will never have enough, will we?"

John wiped the sweat off his brow with his right forearm as he continued driving with his left hand. He took a deep breath and said, "I honestly don't know. It's been so many years like this for us that it's hard to say we'll ever get out of it. Can you remember me saying this fifteen years ago when we met?"

"I sure can."

"You sure can. And you are still hearing me say it now. So, if I'm being honest, I'm not sure it will ever end. But I can only assure you that I'll give it my all and that we can keep trying for as long as possible."

John had his window down as he continued to drive. Fresh and cool air came into the car, and along with the coffee he had drunk when he got up, kept him awake just enough to continue going straight in his lane as he sped along at fifty five miles an hour.

* * *

On the same morning, at the same time, a thirty-year-old blonde woman with natural highlights in her hair was driving in a green van. She was driving southbound on Highway 712. She was leaving Scranton, where her apartment was, and driving to Wilkes-Barre, where her job was. The same radiant sun shone over the Moosic Mountains and into her eyes. She was well-rested and ready for her job as a security guard. As she drove, she spoke to her girlfriend.

"I don't know if my lawyer will do anything about it, Molly," she said in a stern voice.

"But you didn't do anything wrong," Molly replied softly.

"I know I didn't actually *try* to hurt anyone. But you never know how they're going to interpret it in court."

"But Tara, all you did was defend me from an overconfident guy who was not taking any and every hint or direct statement that I could possibly throw at him. How could he end up being the one on the offense, and you wind up being on the defense? It doesn't make any sense."

"No, it doesn't make any sense. However, what I'm starting to learn in Wilkes-Barre is that it does not have to make sense. It doesn't matter what I did or what he did or if he threatened me or threatened you. Nothing matters except for the fact that he is a family friend of the judge. As long as that's the case, I don't have high aspirations for my future."

There was a long pause on the phone and then Molly's soft voice replied. "That sickens me. I can't accept that you could lose your job and possibly even your schooling because some guy hit on me, and you defended me."

As Molly spoke, Tara became angry. She smoked her cigarette fervently and blew big plumes of smoke at the windshield, and after it hit the windshield, it dissipated throughout the vehicle and caused a perpetual fog in it. Her window was cracked so the smoke stayed resident in the air, yet it seeped out a little at a time. She spoke through the Bluetooth in her vehicle, and her phone was on the seat next to her.

"Yeah, every day, I wait as if I'm going to be condemned. I am always anticipating a call from a man I find incompetent and whom I detest to find out my fate. The worst part is that I just want it to be over with, and for it to be over, I need to get that phone call to see if he was able to make a deal or if I'm going to court."

"Tara, I am so sorry my family would not give us the money to get you a real lawyer. I'm so sorry that they are so hateful and unsupportive and that they will not help. What I'm so afraid of is that the public defender isn't going to be able to make the argument or pull the strings that a regular lawyer would, and therefore you're going to be left out to dry before the judge and the defense."

"Well, I'm hoping so much that it does not come to that. I'm hoping the public defender can do his job and just close this ridiculous case for what it is – nothing. I'm putting everything I've got into that, and we will see what happens from there. My fate is up to either a court case or a plea bargain. I don't have very high hopes for either."

"What do you think your job and your college will do if you get a felony or even a misdemeanor for assault?"

Tara responded almost instantly and reflexively. "My job will almost definitely get rid of me. I'm a security guard, honey. There's no way they're going to keep a security guard if I just had a criminal charge of assault. That is something I am positive of because I've seen several people who have applied and got denied solely because of their criminal record. So, this job I have had for nine years is out if I get that charge."

"And school?"

"Who knows? I have been told that colleges have a group who will review a criminal charge if you get one and decide whether you can stay. If I go before that, I don't have high hopes. I highly doubt that they will look kindly upon any violent crime or any kind of infraction involving confrontation with another person. I will probably become a liability for them and they will get rid of me, too."

"Isn't that the opposite of the open-mindedness that any school is supposed to have?"

"It is, but who knows? I have friends who have been unable to get into school because of charges that were a lot less."

Molly began to cry, and her sobs became audible through the phone.

"Don't cry, Molly. I'll figure something out. We'll find a way to make this work for you and me. Even if they slap a felony on me, I'll find some way for us to make it."

"Tara, are you sure about that? Every person I ever knew who had a felony was kept out of just about everything they wanted to do. It's like a scarlet letter, once you have one, you are screwed."

"I know. I have a friend named Melissa who got one, and I saw what it cost her. She lost school, she lost her job, and virtually everything she ever tried to apply to after that was out of reach for her. Life for her just became ceaseless and painful rejection. I know how bad it is. What can I do? There are no options. There's just figuring out a way to make it around the felony if they decide to take me to court and I lose."

As Tara drove on the highway, she inhaled her cigarette very deeply. She lit the next one right after she had finished the previous one, and she used the cherry of the almost finished cigarette to light the new one. She kept her left hand on the bottom of the wheel, and the car continued to fill with smoke.

She looked at the screen on the console at the center of her car. It said there was a detour in fifteen miles due to an accident. She used the hand that held the phone to tap the screen. She altered the trip in such a way as to get around that detour. She held the cigarette in her left hand and continued to hold the wheel with the same hand weakly. As she did so, the car began drifting from her side of the highway's lane and over the double yellow line, where it started to go to the other side of the road.

Highway 712 contained all the brightness of the fall sun shining on it when Tara Simpson's van approached John Matthew's sedan. Neither Tara nor John saw the other person's vehicle until it was too late. Tara was not looking at the road, and John was looking at it but not seeing it due to his immense fatigue and emotional upset.

* * *

It was 7:42 AM when the collision occurred. The crash was head-on, and the sound of the metal of Tara's van striking and bending the front of John's sedan was tremendous. All of the strong and hard materials on both automobiles bent almost instantly. The vehicles were transformed and no longer looked like they were made of alloy or metal but another substance that resembled something malleable like foam or clay.

Tara's green van crashed into the driver's side of John's small and red sedan. John was in the highway's other lane and was holding his cell phone to his head. When Tara's van struck, it hit in such a way that served to plow John's sedan. His car was pushed loudly and violently from his lane of the road into the ravine. As it was pushed into the small valley, it began to tumble on its side. The sound of the accident was abrupt and jarring. All of his and her windows shattered at once in a great cacophony.

Everyone nearby going to Scranton that day on Highway 712 at 7:42 in the morning slammed on their brakes. There were four cars behind John when he was hit and each of them collided with one another. All that could be heard was the loud screeching of the tires as they slid against the asphalt. All of this – the impact, the screeching tires, and the broken windows, served as one great prelude to the horror of the accident.

John heard all of these noises and for several moments each of them struck an unconscious terror into his heart. He heard them and internalized them as the drum beats of death. There was no pain as he turned his head and saw Tara's van collide with his small sedan. There was just shock. There was the stunned state of a man who saw the prospect of his life being torn from him. John had no conscious interest in dying. However, in that briefest of moments, he had the epiphany that he had no choice or control over the possibility of death. He felt one airbag deploy on the side of his car and another from the steering wheel. There was momentary weightlessness and then he felt himself flip over in the vehicle. It was then that he felt nausea enter into his shock. The nausea that he felt was for his existence and it included his dread and anticipation of what dreams may come.

John's sedan tumbled into the ravine. His car rolled over one full-time and then the first part of a second time before it got stuck lying upside down. By the time the vehicle made its first revolution, John was no longer conscious. The last thought in his mind was of his daughter, Isabella. He saw her delicate little face and her blue eyes and the image of that visage carried him into an uncertain unconsciousness.

The smell of smoke, carbon monoxide, gas, and oil surrounded him. There was a hissing noise from his sedan and the wheels were still spinning as he lay in the great arena that he so often imagined Scranton to be.

Tara had no conception that she had lost control of the van until the moment she hit John's vehicle. Her airbag went off instantaneously and her head slammed into it with a sudden fury. Her van served as a battering ram for John's car and panic consumed her mind.

Tara understood this feeling of helplessness and alienation in her life. In these moments of terror and angst, she suddenly felt these feelings become greatly amplified. She felt an utter lack of agency and control that she had fiercely fought against since she was an adolescent. Any disintegration of agency in Tara's existence illuminated the tremendous anxieties of these pathologies of the past. Yet again, she found herself awaiting a future to be determined by foreign and uncontrollable forces. She knew that this time it might mean her life. As the airbag collided violently with her face, she instantly tasted blood before it knocked her into unconsciousness.

All that could be heard was the hum of industry in the surrounding Scranton town as movement on the highway ceased. Each person in the accident lay unconscious and their cars were motionless. Highway 712 came to a complete stop.

Peter Wang was amongst the other individuals who slammed on the brakes behind John and Tara.

He was shaken up by it. He removed his glasses from his face, massaged his brow, and pushed his thin dark hair off his forehead. Peter was on his way to his job at Scranton University as a computer programmer. He pulled his cell phone out of his pocket and called 911 for the emergency.

"Hello, I would like to report an accident. At least six vehicles are involved," Peter said, and his voice sounded shaken.

"Okay, sir. Were you one of the vehicles that were involved?"

"Yes. But I am okay. There are two main cars involved. The rest of us collided by slamming on the brakes due to their accident."

"Where are you located?"

"I am northbound on Highway 712 going to Scranton. I am about two miles or so from the college."

The conversation proceeded, and dispatch was sent immediately. By 9:56, John, Tara, and another driver were being treated. Special equipment was needed to get John out of his car.

As John and Tara were taken away in the ambulance, a group of police officers began directing traffic so that the highway was clear and the commerce of the day was allowed to continue. Within two hours, the glass was cleaned up, the cars were moved, and there was no hint or suggestion that an accident had ever occurred.

CHAPTER 1

LANGUAGE

I felt an odd but wonderful excitement well up inside me when I awoke. The accident occurred and my last thought was my daughter and then the next thing I knew I was in a strange new land. There was a woman who spoke softly and said her name was Sophia. She approached me and we walked together. When she came toward me, any fear I felt just sort of... melted away. I became sort of like a newborn baby looking in all directions as if I were just discovering the world anew. I was standing on the ground of what looked like a great city all around me. There was something overwhelming for me as I looked at the city. It was the way one feels when they are looking down from a cliff at a beautiful ravine or canyon. The wonderment of the city tickled every one of my senses. I felt like a child accidentally stumbling upon Arcadia, Utopia, or even Eden itself.

There was an intoxicating smell of the forest as we both stood together. Sophia nodded to me and we began our journey into the city. The aroma of the forest was replaced by an equally intoxicating fragrance. Every time it filled my lungs, I smelled a certain scent... it was like some heavenly food. But the more I smelled it, I recognized that it wasn't food. It was just a delicious smell. It smelled in such a way that made my mouth water and my stomach growl all at once until I got used to it. That's what I meant when I said it smelled like food. I didn't even have to ask Sophia about it.

But let me go on – the smell isn't really important. Let it suffice to say it smelled good. I kept up side by side with Sophia, and my head twisted back and forth and all around the whole time. I was so curious about everything and tried to analyze everything I saw and heard.

The first thing I saw when I entered the city was a train – well, it looked like a train – a large, white structure gliding by us on tracks. I could see in its windows that there were lots of people inside each passenger carriage. After it passed, there were paths and mountains and hills and houses, too – just like here – and yet it all was somehow different. It was like every building in sight had architecture, the likes of which I'd never seen before. I'd seen all the styles separately... but never together like they were on the buildings I saw here. There were things about the architecture that looked Greek, some that looked Roman, some were Chinese-looking, and some that I'd seen in ancient Persian history books. Other facets of the buildings looked from the Middle Ages and others looked modern... I could see Russian and Middle Eastern, European and North American influences, South American and Australian influences, and even a bunch I couldn't recognize, too, all at once. It was as if every building... every *structure* in the city had a little piece of each culture in the world on it somewhere. And it was *beautiful*. There'd be a building with white marble columns in the front and bamboo for the curtains in the window and a turret on the side – all those different styles right next to each other. And then the building next to it would contain three *different* styles – or maybe four or five – just like that, every building!

Sophia and I kept walking, and I could see she was just letting me take it all in. She looked straight ahead, and every now and then, I could see her turn her head toward me out of the corner of my eye. And then I'd see her grin. She'd smile a big beautiful smile and then turn her head forward again to look straight ahead as we walked.

The sun was shining, and it was as bright as can be in the city, too. As I adjusted to the physical differences – the architecture and its diversity – I became aware of other differences. For instance, it was oddly quiet for a city. That isn't to say it wasn't full of life – it was. There were adults and kids all around. The inhabitants surrounded Sophia and I on all sides. They were out and about doing all manner of things, but somehow, it was quieter. Their machines – lawnmowers, weed whackers, and others didn't screech and scream like ours, and the train or bus or whatever you want to call the vehicle I saw on the way in, glided by with a smoothness and ease that, although audible, did not offend the ear. The entire city seemed quiet and peaceful and wonderful. All I *could* hear was their voices, the sounds of animals, and the cool wind occasionally brushing past my ears – but nothing else, no... no noises of industrialization, you know?

They looked just like us for the most part. Same heights. Same basic weights, the whole deal. The only difference I could really see on a surface level was that they all seemed to have a different and pretty vibrant skin color.

It became obvious after only a few moments that they were all part of the same race – the race Sophia was. They had dark, bronze-colored skin. As I watched and examined them, I noticed it was universal – every one of them – had bronze-colored skin. But some had a lighter tint, and others had a darker shade to their complexion. But I couldn't see any distinctions based on it. I didn't ask Sophia, but now that I'm thinking about it, I'm pretty certain there weren't any distinctions. Some lighter-tinted men were with the darker-tinted women as they passed us on the road in their cars, and some darker-tinted men were with lighter-tinted women, too.

We'd pass by younger children alongside the path, and there were no distinctions there, either. Everyone mingled together no matter how light or dark their bronze-colored tint was... there seemed to be no social status based on any variations, or at least nothing I could detect. I guess it was sort of like the way their architecture was – varied but together – diverse but unified, you know?

I wondered if they would speak to me. I thought they could see me by the look in their eyes, but would they talk to me? This was the first thing I asked Sophia since we had left the elevated part of the clouds. I could hear the people talking to each other as we walked by, but I couldn't make head nor tail of what they were saying. So, I turned to Sophia,

"Are they speaking English Sophia? Are they speaking English like us, and I just can't hear them clearly enough?"

Sophia turned her head toward me and I watched as the sun continued illuminating the greenest and most beautiful eyes I ever saw in my life.

"The Amoenians have come to realize that language is the keystone of communication and since we are social beings, it is, then, one of the keystones of unification. The need for a universal language was imperative when we agreed to dissolve the divisiveness of nations. We also realized that it would be unfair to use one established lexicon while disregarding all the others. That is why we agreed to compromise. We constructed a lexicon that is a hybrid of all the world's *major* languages. There is only one language now and it is used by everyone."

I just looked at her in confusion.

"You see," she continued, "the human faculty for language is simply astounding, as scientist after scientist has shown over the ages. At a young age, the brain is capable of learning a seemingly limitless set of morphemes and phonemes that compose words. That is why the Amoenians decided not to restrict this incredible human faculty. We took the idea from English. English is so beautiful in large part due to the fact that it combines morphemes from so many different languages – such as Latin, the Germanic languages, French, and others. That is why before Amoenish, English was the major language with the largest lexicon – because it combined the morphemes of other languages and made them into a sort of uber-language, if you will. The Amoenians took this concept from English and used it to make one language out of all the major languages. We created a lexicon that incorporates all of the languages in the world into a single idiom that is used to connect us all. In a single Amoenish sentence, English, German, Chinese, Russian, and African terms may be utilized."

I nodded. It seemed simple enough to me.

"The Amoenish language has only certain broad lexical rules for the formation of its sentences – similar to the English rule for declarative sentences being subject-verb-predicate. We, as a people, decided on this grammatical structure. These rules of lexical chronology formed the most logical order of a declarative sentence, so we implemented the rule into Amoenish. And every Amoenian knows this grammatical structure because it is taught in every Amoenian school – by global law. The terms used to fill this subject-verb-predicate linguistic structure in an Amoenish sentence are almost limitless. In fact, John, the Amoenish dictionary is incredibly large and our children are rigorously schooled in vocabulary early in their education – when their minds are most adept for the acquisition of grammatical rules. You see, every word has at least one synonym, something like in English, only many times broader. The synonyms in Amoenian are a compilation of all human language's terms for the same concepts. For instance, take the word, 'unify.' In English, the words that mean unify are, 'consolidate,' 'unite,' 'combine,' 'amalgamate,' 'coalesce,' 'bring together,' 'fuse,' 'join,' 'weld,' 'merge,' 'confederate,' 'incorporate,' and 'integrate.' But in Amoenish, there are many other terms one can use to mean, 'unify.' For example, Spanish's *unificar*, the French *unifier*, the 成一体 of simplified Chinese, Russian's унифицировать, German's *vereinheitlichen*, the Dutch term *verenigen*, and many others are all acceptable terms for 'to unify' in Amoenish. You see, John?"

I nodded in amazement.

"So, then," Sophia continued, "for each idea, a veritable litany of terms are taught and learned."

"But it must be impossible to learn, Sophia," I objected.

"You underestimate a child's faculty for knowledge, John. It is remarkably simple for most children to pick up, especially since so many of the morphemes are the same across languages. For example, as you can with unified, the 'uni' morpheme is the same in English, French, Spanish, and Italian. The 'vere' morpheme is the same in Dutch and German languages. You understand?"

"Yes."

"Good. Throughout the early years of a child's development, Amoenish vocabulary is taught relentlessly so that *all* of us – every person – is linked by a basic language. It is what we call a global mandate. Needless to say, the wealth of words makes the language very conducive to the rhyme and meter of the bard and the prose of the dramatist."

"A global mandate?"

"Yes, John," she said, but then immediately waved her hand towards me, "but we are getting ahead of ourselves. I will explain that later. Now come on."

We continued walking, and I watched a little boy kicking a ball in a group of other Amoenians. The smell of food – or whatever was making my stomach growl, gave way to a sweet-smelling scent like that of flowers. I decided to ask Sophia the most obvious question that came to mind.

"But you only speak English Sophia. If Amoenish is as encompassing as you say, how come you are only speaking to me in English?"

"The purpose of language is, above all, communication. I need to communicate with you, John. And so, I am limiting my lexicon for your benefit. Let me give an example of how, they," she pointed to the Amoenians kicking the small blue ball, "are speaking and how I usually speak. If I were speaking to you in Amoenish, the statement, 'I am taking you to see the delight that is our city,' may sound like this;

'Yo presa di 見るため a zie наслаждение _ 是 norte city,' and any Amoenian would understand instantly because they have learned the different words all their life, and the structure of our sentences – the basic grammatical rules – remain the same. Each lexical slot in a sentence may be filled with a large number of terms, all of which have the same basic meaning. We only agree on the *rules* of language – and they are basic, logical, and agreed upon. This large lexicon is learned young, and the average Amoenian has no problem picking it up in their formative years. Of course, in each local peoplement, the lexicon that is utilized is slightly different, some more heavily favoring English, others more heavily favoring Latin, and so on, but no local peoplement in all of Amoena Vieta uses exclusively one language – unless that language is Amoenish – all languages."

I stood speechless as I looked at the Amoenians laughing, talking and kicking the ball, and I suddenly felt like a pilgrim in an unknown land. Sophia saw my fear and consternation rise and quickly comforted me,

"But do not worry, John. The Amoenians have the capacity to isolate any single lexicon and will adapt to be understood. I promise to speak to you in the beauty of English and nothing else."

"Thank you, Sophia," I said gratefully and my body untensed immediately. "But why – why do you use language this way?"

"Because language is implicit in the formation of thought. Thoughts cannot be limited in a good and just society. So, then, by enabling Amoenians to utilize the lexicon of many languages, it allows them to think more fully and create – to express themselves more fully as human beings."

"But don't people still speak the language they are more comfortable with, predominantly or entirely? What I mean is, don't some families or groups speak

English to each other, while others speak Spanish with no other lexicons utilized?"

Sophia did not hesitate before responding, "Of course, John. That is only human nature. Many groups speak almost entirely Russian or Chinese, Latin or English, with the addendum that all the words spoken are in the subject-verb-predicate order. And it does not matter if some small groups choose to isolate one idiom's terms because they understand every other lexicon since they learned all the terms when they were young and continue learning the terms via mass media. We ensure they all have a working vocabulary by testing the young generations each year rigorously. Language is of utmost importance to Amoenians, John. We understand its importance and its power. It enables us to communicate – to know one another. It's the language that serves as the conduit for us to live together side by side," she said, and we continued walking the gravel path into the city. I continued looking at the panorama of architecture in awe and at the people who looked and acted so much like us.

"Now let's get a move on, John," she spoke softly, "We have a big day ahead of us. The first thing I want to show you is the capital. That is where we are headed now."

And with that, we continued walking and talking about the wonderment that is Amoena Vieta. Sophia continued to walk on my side – never in front or behind. She reached out and softly tugged my arm to direct me to our next destination. I walked with a confidence that only trust can make one feel as we navigated the gravel path and entered the capital.

CHAPTER 2

THE SOCIETAL COVENANT
AND GLOBAL SERVICEMENT

The different parts of the city that Sophia and I walked through varied as widely as the first sections I described to you earlier. The different people we passed varied immensely by height and their personal presentation style... the way they walked, how they talked, the clothes they wore, and so on.

People were scattered along the path – many on it and many in the yards and coming out of the buildings on either side. Some Amoenians passed by on foot and others in little scooter-esque vehicles that made a soft buzzing sound and didn't move much faster than walking. We passed many people on foot, as there were constantly people on the paths throughout Amoena Vieta speaking in all those strange languages I couldn't recognize. Still others jogged by with large wet rings of sweat showing through their shirts and some jogged by without shirts at all, exposing their upper bodies. I guess you could say it was like a nicer version of a city street.

It's sort of like I said about the air... it was... cleaner, fresher, and better for the lungs. In fact,

Amoena Vieta was cleaner, fresher, and better for all the senses. The atmosphere was in some way more conducive for the soul. It was kind of like the difference between drinking tap water and purified water: just all-around fresher. I remember that very well. It was a pleasure to inhale deeply and let all the pure air rush into my lungs and fill them with exhilaration and it was a pleasure to let my eyes feast on the terrain, letting my brain just brim with excitement. For instance, there were no hamburger wrappers, crushed beer cans, broken bottles or dirty tissues lining the path. There were no cigarette butts all over the place, no big ugly smokestacks filling the air with foul-smelling smoke, and no chimneys burping gaseous refuse out of the houses, either. It was *completely* different from here – and yet, at the same time, so much the same.

I became pensive after experiencing all of this before me. To be honest, I'm not entirely certain how they kept it so clean in every meaning of the term "clean." I suddenly became serious and felt the stubble on my cheeks and chin as I paused for a few more moments. Then the consternation vanished from my face and I could not figure out how a place that was clearly very populated could be so devoid of any pollution. It wasn't long before I got my answer.

As Sophia and I walked to the capital of Amoena Vieta, we saw all kinds of Amoenians, doing all manner of things... just like I said. But I forgot to mention that amongst the Amoenians, there were groups who worked alongside the path every couple of miles – or yards – I can't really measure the distance in my memory. In fact, everywhere I went with Sophia, there were these groups of Amoenians who *weren't* dressed uniquely – but instead were all in black uniform shirts. At first, I thought they must be the Amoenians's version of road construction workers. I noticed that there was always a group of black-shirted people working and a bunch of green-shirted people watching them closely. But as I looked closer, I realized the black-shirted men weren't doing road work at all. They were just picking up garbage and brushing the rocks on the path so that they were evenly spread. I saw others who were cleaning the street signs with a rag. Then, there were still other groups holding up little, square, white machines that make a "swoosh" sound like how our leaf suckers do.

"Who are they?" I asked Sophia after I walked past several members of the group.

"The black-shirted groups are what you would call prisoners, John."

"Right out in the open like this?"

"Yes. The Amoenians don't let those who have broken society's laws simply linger in a cell allowing their human power to atrophy. We put their abilities to use by letting them do work that benefits all of our commonwealth," she said, and I noticed a slightly irritated look glide across her face. "But don't worry about them yet, John. I'll get to explaining how our criminal justice system works later – I promise I will."

I didn't say another word about it until we got to the capital building, but I watched each group closely whenever we passed one. They were sparsely set up – and always in little groups of three or four people. I was dying to ask more about them, but after seeing the slight irritation on Sophia's face, I felt I should do whatever I could not to make her upset. So, I didn't rock the boat and take a chance on missing out on any aspect of Amoena Vieta that Sophia wanted to share with me.

Another thing I noticed as we walked to the capital was that while all the buildings and houses that lined the streets were different in shape, architecture, and decoration, none of them were exceedingly tall compared to all the others. It was the same with the houses. They were all different, with a character of their own – some shaped like one of our regular bi-level houses – and yet others had square masonry like the ones you see in pictures of houses in Italy.

Still, others were similar to the way a Spanish pueblo looks. And there were about a hundred other designs – no two were the same. But none of the buildings towered above all the rest, you know? No building had *everything,* while others had nothing. It was sort of like they were; "different but equal."

Sophia and I walked by building after building along the main path. There were constantly little paths veering off the main track, but Sophia always kept us on the main path, and everywhere we went that sweet-smelling air surrounded us and that warm, delightful sun blessed our heads. The atmosphere in the city was such that I didn't really notice it must have taken a great long time for us to get there – but throughout the trip, I admittedly had no real concept of time. I had no gauge for it and no desire to think about it. In fact, that was the only thing that wasn't completely realistic about my time in Amoena Vieta – the lack of time. Everything else was so similar to home. I kept looking for something to suggest it was surreal, but it was as real as anything I've ever experienced.

Before I knew it Sophia pointed ahead of us and began speaking,

"Welcome to our capital, John," she said in a more formal voice, sort of how a tour guide repeats her script. "We are delighted to have you, and we accept your arrival with open arms." Then flashed her bright, perfect smile and I remember it almost knocked me over because of how beautiful her face was.

* * *

The capital building Sophia pointed to was not set off from the buildings that lined it on the right and left of the path. A road ran right in front of it, and there was a small glass room – a vestibule similar to our bus terminals – in the back. The building was made of white masonry and it was only a couple of levels high. The only really distinguishing feature of the capital building Sophia took me to when I compared it to all the other structures I'd seen was that it had a giant statue of two large, white marble hands on the top that looked as if they were sculpted by Michelangelo himself. The two enormous hands were embracing each other in a sort of eternal hand-shake. Once I saw them, I stood frozen in awe. After a few moments, Sophia noticed that I was no longer by her side. She turned and began to speak,

"John... why'd you stop?"

"It's – it's so different than ours."

Sophia smiled broadly. "That's just the tip of the iceberg, John. Come on, let me show you," she said as she walked back to me and gently touched my arm. I instantly came out of my momentary trance and resumed walking. Before I knew it, we were across what looked like a freshly cut, green lawn that lay between the building and the road, and we came to the front door.

The door was seven or eight feet high and was made of what looked to me like a giant slab of limestone. On it were words that were carved in all the different languages – in Amoenish. I could recognize they were the English words "right" and "freedom" and the Spanish words "bebida" and "consciencia."

"Bebida" means drink, and "consciencia" means conscience. All the words in other languages I couldn't make out, though. Each statement was numbered using Roman numerals, and there were fifteen of them in total. I asked Sophia what it meant, and I saw a joyful eagerness enter her face as she began to speak.

"These are what the Amoenians call the Eternal Rights of the Societal Covenant. They are posted on the doors of the global *servicement's* capital, which is where we stand."

I just raised one eyebrow at the word: "servicement."

"That's the term we use for what you call a government, John. We call it a *servicement* because our government is not merely a government in the traditional sense of the word, but a government run *entirely* by the people being governed, and formed on the basis of providing *services* to those it belongs to – the people. The term, government, automatically gives the entity a foreign sense – a-them-versus-us mentality. We saw no need to make it a foreign entity; no need to call it something that for generations has been associated with enmity amongst people. Put simply: our government is not governed by anyone except the people and its function is service. Therefore, it is the servicement. Understand?"

I nodded.

"Good. The Eternal Rights are also posted on the capital building of every *local peoplement*, which is a smaller version of the global servicement, throughout Amoena Vieta. These rights are the basis of our societal covenant. They also serve as the way for our democratic society to protect the minority – because we recognize that democracy may only serve 51% of the community. The Eternal Rights are a way of ensuring the liberties of the other 49%. Therefore, they are the only code that cannot be changed by a mere majority of the people. These are the rights that also form the basis of our legal system and are known by rote by all Amoenians via their education."

"Can you read them to me?" I asked, bursting with curiosity.

Sophia took a deep breath and began reading them in a calm, proud voice,

"The Eternal Rights of the
Societal Covenant of Amoenians"

I.   "The right to thine own self be true, that is,
       the right to free expression."

       I couldn't help but smile at hearing
       Shakespeare's words make their way into this
       society. His words were the ultimate state-
       ment of authenticity. Sophia continued,

II.   "The right to adequate food and drink, to be
       determined by what the average consump-
       tion of necessities are at any given time.

III.   The right to health care, life, and liberty.

IV.   The prohibition of slavery.

V.   The prohibition of torture.

VI.   The right to a fair trial.

VII.   The right to freedom of thought and conscience.

VIII. The right to freely assemble and associate.

IX.   The right to be free of institutional discrimi-
       nation.

X.   The right to a free and open press.

XI.   The right to petition the global servicement
       and local peoplements.

XII.   The right to an education.

XIII. The right to accessible information and
       knowledge of all public information.

XIV.   The right to rate and participate in all facets
       of the commonweal."

When she finished voicing the fourteenth right, I stood in utter amazement at their utterly humanistic doctrine. The rights seemed so just and fair and complete. Sophia gave me a few moments after the admiration bursting within me subsided, and I finally began to speak,

"Are these rights unalienable? I mean, they can't be revoked?"

"They are almost universally seen as rights that no human being can go without and take an entire 98% of the popular vote to be changed. These rights are not withheld even to those who commit the most grievous crimes against society, John. Amoenians generally believe these rights are not the gift of society... but the gift of birth and the fruit of being part of a good human society. They are unalienable so long as one exists and are the only aspect of Amoenian culture that is nearly un-editable."

A new wave of disbelief washed over me. "Not even to those in prison?"

Sophia smiled like a tolerant mother. "Prison is much different here than where you're from, John. But to answer your question – no, none of the unalienable rights can be eradicated, even in prison. Prisoners' rights can be diminished because they broke the societal covenant. But Amoena Vieta is a place of forgiveness and humanity. No one ever loses their rights altogether because for the people to take one's rights away altogether would be for the people to play God – and that is a role the people cannot play," she said. She reached for the handle on the door that displayed The Eternal Rights, "Now come on, John," she continued and waved her left hand in such a way as to urge me out of my stunned stupor and through the door into the capital.

I got a hold of myself and promptly entered, bringing all the utter curiosity and wonder along with me.

* * *

The inside of the capital was as plain and unadorned as the outside. The floors were white marble and clean and they emitted a lemony-wax sort of smell that made the whole gigantic room pleasant to breathe in. I'd say that there were around a thousand people or maybe even more in the elongated, oval room in which we stood.

Let me restate that for accuracy. All the buildings were very similar, but the capital building was deeper. It was like all the other buildings from the front – from the outside. But from the outside, I couldn't see how deep the capital building was. I could see the depth once I got inside – and as I said, it was gigantic. I'll tell you, it must have been a couple of football fields deep. The seats inside the rectangular structure were arranged in a stretched out oval form – a complete circle, sort of like the seats in a football stadium, except that no seat was elevated above the others. What I mean is, it wasn't like a movie theatre where the rows get higher or anything. We were all on the same level. Honestly, there was no *need* for inclined seating. I mean, everyone could see the most important screens since they were elevated.

Sophia took me to the back of the enormous room, and we sat next to the Amoenians there, on the furthest end of the oval arrangement. Each Amoenian sat in a chair and had a laptop computer on their lap. Some of them were using the computer, looking completely lost in it, and others were talking to each other. But most were looking slightly upward at the top of the room, where four giant screens were hanging down from the ceiling, sort of like the jumbotrons at a football game. All the seats in the entire room were padded with a soft, plushy blue material and were about as comfortable as any seat I'd ever sat in. I listened attentively to the myriad of Amoenish being spoken between the people, and Sophia did not disturb my meandering curiosity. But my wonder only gave way to more wonder, and before long, I began to ask her the whats, whys, and wherefores...

"What's going on here, Sophia? Are these all..." I waved my hand toward the thousands of people in the giant room, "representatives of the people?"

"No," she said, above the discourse of the many Amoenians. "There are no global servicement representatives here. They remain in the local peoplements they represent. You see, Amoenians believe any representative of a group must live in the same area of the people she or he is representing. Living amongst one's constituents motivates a representative to continuously represent the people – because they are no longer abstractions in a faraway place. They are living, breathing beings right in front of the representative every day. All representatives must live amongst those whom they represent in Amoena Vieta. That is why all matters of global servicement business are done by the representative via the computer – via the internet.

"But I digress, John. Let me get back to explaining our global servicement. The room you see before you is filled with about a thousand concerned Amoenians at any given time. The thousand are composed of whoever wants to come, and they can freely come and go as they wish. They are here to oversee the global servicement firsthand, making certain it is ensuring the distribution of global minimums throughout local peoplements. That is one of the three responsibilities the global servicement is charged with – to oversee the local peoplements, making positive they are distributing the global minimums of goods and services to all people. The second responsibility of global servicement is peacekeeping between local peoplements – making certain no violent factions form within their own local peoplement. And the third is also oversight... to ensure that the Eternal Rights are being upheld."

As I looked over the enormous rectangular room, I didn't know what to ask first. The throngs of people I saw before me were overwhelming. My eyes kept wandering to the thousand blinking screens of the laptops, though. "Why do they all sit in front of a computer?" I asked Sophia.

Sophia's arm raised and pointed ahead without her saying a thing. I followed her long, extended finger pointing to the large circle of screens at the top of the room. On the screen, I saw all sorts of names, words and numbers I could not understand.

"Our systems of servicement and peoplement," Sophia said, "both globally and locally, hinge on the premise of democracy – of *people* rule. Democracy is one of the truly beautiful systems we retained from the earlier civilizations because of its emphasis on the empowerment of the individual. But while the earlier democracies almost all gradually became corrupted by oligarchical rule and, little by little, excluded the *people* from having the power – the Amoenians disabled even the *possibility* of oligarchical rule."

I looked at Sophia in a daze of confusion because she did not answer my question at all. I asked why they all had computers, and she went on about oligarchies and democracy.

"You see John, civilization needed to find a way to guard against the oligarchy. Even in a representative democracy, we saw that oligarchies were possible since the people place all the power of servicement into their representative's hands. Only the invention and then relative perfection of the computer enabled a true democracy to thrive. The internet functions as the material link that connects us all. Once we were able to create safeguards against corruption and misuse, the internet turned into a staple of our civilization. It allows us to truly give the power of servicement back to the people – to *all* the people. Everyone in the world, John – *everyone* – owns a computer as a birthright and is obligated to participate in both the global and local commonweal.

"The problem of representatives not being responsible for the people until the next election cycle became a thing of the past with the advent of the computer. It is the internet that allows the people to serve as a veto power on the global servicement and local peoplement's activities. Every activity of servicement is monitored by parts of the population at all times. In fact," she lifted her finger and pointed toward the giant, square screen, "the screen you see in front of us contains a list of all the local peoplement oversights that are taking place right now throughout the entirety of Amoena Vieta. That is global servicement's most important job, John – to conduct oversight and make certain that global minimums are being distributed. Millions of Amoenians are right this moment actively logged onto their elected representative's servicement-oversight dealings webpage to see how well their representative is doing at coordinating oversight in their local peoplement. All actions a representative takes are posted on her or his internet site by a chosen citizen from that local peoplement. Whenever their representative puts forth or tries to execute a rule for local peoplement oversight that they do not condone, the citizens of that local peoplement have the power to veto it. If enough of the local peoplements's population vetoes the action, the oversight rule that the representative put forth or tried to execute is stopped instantaneously. That is the reason for the computers you asked about and that is also the reason for the giant monitor you see before us. Computers enabled us to create a more perfect democracy: a happy medium between a representative democracy and a direct democracy. The global minimums are determined by direct democracy – everyone must vote on them. But on the majority of issues, our democracy is a representative democracy wherein the *people* have veto power on the legislation passed by global service-ment."

"But how can the people possibly oversee the inner workings of the global servicement all the time and still work and have lives of their own, Sophia? Isn't it too impractical?"

"No, John, you don't understand," she said as she gently put her warm hand on my shoulder, "The global servicement's voting procedures are only active for a short period of time each year. Its entire role of legislation is setting base minimums of goods and services that all people are entitled to."

"Like a minimum wage of goods and services, you mean?"

"Very much like that, John. A base minimum which all people are entitled by the Eternal Rights. The global servicement gets its orders from the people during that short time – four weeks that every Amoenian is given off from work, so it *obligates* to participate in the global commonweal during the time the global minimums are set. The global minimums affect every person, and so they are determined by direct democracy. The rest of the year, the global representative mainly coordinates the oversight of the local peoplement's distribution of minimums by ensuring that the local peoplements are provid-ing all of the set minimums for all the people of the local peoplement. In other words, the global servicement is primarily an overseer of the local peoplement. Throughout the year, the representatives take people's orders and continue to monitor the local peoplements using community groups. The global representatives are also responsible for ensuring that no local peoplement is becoming a faction or oligarchy that is imposing its rule on other local peoplements. If the elected representatives fail their constituents in any one of these responsibilities, they are removed and replaced by the people of their local peoplements at any time. This ensures they are responsible for the people in their local peoplements at all times."

"I see," I said as I tried to understand, "What you are saying, then, is that the global servicement is responsible for ensuring that the local peoplement is, at all times, fulfilling its responsibilities to the people?"

Sophia smiled broadly. "Precisely John. You are beginning to understand. The Amoenians believe very strongly in the necessity of checks and balances. The idea permeates all aspects of our peoplement because it is a staple for ensuring the common good."

It was an incredible sight and process. Truthfully, it left me in awe. In Amoena Vieta, the people are the president. What I mean is that there are still representatives who pass legislation, like in the U.S. and other similar systems, but there is no president there with the power to veto. Instead, in Amoena

Vieta, *the people* assume the presidential responsibility insofar as legislation is concerned. The people have the veto power over the process.

However, for major issues like these *global minimums* that Sophia kept mentioning, the servicement is unlike ours in that it becomes a direct democracy. The *popular* vote is what sets those global minimums.

I thought about all these concepts for a few moments. Then I looked at Sophia and asked, "Do all nations work this way in Amoena Vieta?"

Sophia laughed like a tolerant teacher with an imbecile for a student. "There are no nations, John. There are only human beings. All facets of human diversity are tolerated in Amoena Vieta – self-expression, religions, philosophies, and so on. But the Amoenians recognize the eternal truth that we are all human beings – not members of merely any family or country – but of the human family and the world country that is Amoena Vieta. We understand that the differences between us do not necessitate any hierarchy of human worth. Every heart beats the same way – we are forever linked and responsible to our humanity, not our land. That is why Amoenians generally believe in one large humanistic association of human beings – for the good of all. This is not formed from a religious or philosophical belief, although it can be found in many religions. The unifying sentiment is generally regarded as an eternal and fairly obvious truth that is needed for the cultivation of a good society. Cultivating a feeling of universal camaraderie is the only way we believe we can create a good world for all. Ever since the dawn of humanity, every truly great thinker has agreed with our assertion of this eternal truth. It is imbibed by all the young in Amoenian schools and is cultivated throughout the education of life."

A flood of questions made their way to the consciousness of my mind, even despite being distracted by the constantly changing large screens, the cacophony of voices and that purifying smell of lemon that drifted throughout the room. I sat there thinking, trying to choose one above the others. Sophia saw my pensive hesitance and spoke up,

"You can ask me questions on the way, John. But for now, we must go. Once I show you the functionality of a local peoplement, I think you will understand better. Come on, let us go."

And with that, she got up, moved in front of me, and began walking toward the door on which was printed the Eternal Rights. I took one last look over the sea of interested faces, most of which stared at the screens in front of us. Then I got up and quickly caught up with Sophia as she walked out the door.

CHAPTER 3

TRANSPORTATION, RELIGION, AND THE LOCAL PEOPLEMENT

We left the capital building and walked side by side. The sun blessed our bodies with its warm caress. I broke the silence between us,

"Where are we going?"

"To a local peoplement so you can see," Sophia replied almost instantly.

We walked for what seemed a mile or two. Several times along the way, I saw the transport zip near us through breaks in the trees and the houses on either side of the path. The warm, clean, breezy air seemed to hover throughout Amoena Vieta, filling my lungs and I could not refrain from periodically smiling in delight. In the distance, all around us, I could hear the constant, soft voices of the people dotted with the soothing sound of children's laughter. The two sounds mixed together, creating a calming sort of cadence similar to the mingling sounds of crickets and frogs at night in the country. And that delicious smell – I still can't put my finger on it – continued to drift throughout the land like an invisible but welcome fog, spilling into my nose and intoxicating me the way an expensive perfume teases and flirts with the nostrils.

We continued walking alongside the gravel path and progressed to an ever greener, more pastoral part of the land. On each side of the path, there was still a line of diverse architectural houses as far as the eye could see. But reaching over the houses like wooded giants were different, larger, more impressive trees than any I'd seen earlier on the path, and alongside many of the houses grew a maze of dark green ivy that served as a kind of outline to the different architectures of the houses, enhancing their beauty.

And I noticed that some of what I thought were houses weren't really houses at all. I saw people walking into some of the structures and coming out with bags in their hands. That's when I realized many of the structures – or at least some – were actually little shops along the wide gravel path. I didn't even ask Sophia about it. It was too obvious and I would have just felt silly.

Sophia didn't say anything as we walked. She just kept by my side, allowing my senses to take it all in without distraction. Every so often, out of the corner of my eye, I'd see her glance over at me. But she'd never say anything. She'd only grin and continue walking.

A little before we arrived at the transport station she was taking me to, I saw the first life other than human life in the great city. Two red birds similar to cardinals, but more beautiful, streaked across the sky overhead. And I'm telling you, they took my breath away. And just before arriving at the transport station, I saw a bunch of children outside, playing some sort of game I couldn't recognize, laughing and screaming and having what looked to me like a really good time. There were two groups of the little ones and they stood across a yard from each other and threw a ball back and forth. And this big brown dog that looked like a cocker-spaniel ran back and forth after the ball each time one group threw it, then the other. The dog seemed to be ceaselessly and eagerly waiting for one of the groups of children to botch the catch so it could claim the prize as its own.

Finally, we reached a large, grey cement structure that looked like an oversized dugout. People were going in and out through two large revolving doors in the front. Before I knew it, Sophia was pulling me by my arm through the revolving doors and into the building.

"This is a transport station, John," she told me as we entered the structure. The inside was sparsely adorned, with blue walls and a grey cement floor. It was something like the capital building but it was *much* bigger on the inside than it looked to be from the outside. But instead of being deep like the capital building, the transport station building was low – the floor was many feet below the ground. So, in the front it looked small, but in actuality, it wasn't.

I briefly glanced around the entirety of the transport station's main room. People were all over the inside... coming, going, rushing, talking. Some carried bags and papers with them while others didn't have a single item in their hands. I felt sort of like I was at the airport. There were people behind long counters in front of the room, talking to other Amoenians. There were several large screens – smaller versions of those in the capital building – all around the room with text sprawled all over them. I saw that many of the people in there – fifty or sixty people, I'd say – were constantly glancing up at them, then looking down at the papers in their hands.

"Everyone in each local peoplement uses the transport centers stationed throughout the local peoplement – usually three or four – to travel any distance. Each transport center has a certain route, and in every local peoplement, there are transport centers that are able to take anyone to any part of any local peoplement. If one needs to go to another peoplement, they can go to a transport center that will take them to an inter-transport center in the next local peoplement. Virtually all of Amoena

Vieta – the whole world, is interconnected by the transports. And every single human being is free to travel anywhere they choose on these transport centers. What I'm getting at, John, is that travel is both free and encouraged in Amoena Vieta. It is not limited to the wealthy or the privileged. We feel it is everyone's world, and since the world belongs to all, all have a right to see it. Perhaps even more importantly, the public transport system also preserves the beauty of our environment by eliminating the vast amount of fuel waste along with the pollution emitted by each citizen having their own vehicle."

I didn't understand the Amoenian system at first. It seemed to me that it was too limited. As I watched the hustle and bustle all around in the large room, I asked, "But what about the times that the bus –" I caught myself, "the transports are running? Don't the schedules of the transports make it incredibly inconvenient for the individual?"

Sophia let out a loud but tolerant laugh. "No, John. We have a transport station system where transports run continuous loops throughout the local peoplement. It is timed so that every ten minutes a new transport arrives and makes the trip around the local peoplement following the route of the preceding transport. The transports hit most major areas of a city and therefore the walk from wherever the transport stops will be minimal. Some prefer mopeds or scooters to eliminate the walk altogether, but that is rare. It is far healthier and better to walk, and generally, those who can, do."

"I see. But what about an emergency?" I asked, "Like when someone has a heart attack or something and *can't* wait ten minutes for the next transport?"

"In the event of an emergency, personal transport is sent directly to the needed destination. There are a sufficient number of personal transports ready and waiting for emergency phone calls."

I nodded in awe, and Sophia promptly walked up to the front desk to speak with one of the Amoenians there. She talked to them for a few minutes. A little while later, Sophia returned with a ticket, and before I knew it, we were on a transport.

The transport was almost exactly like a bus spliced with a train. It was really long and narrow so it could fit tons of people. There were two sets – two rows of cushioned box seats that could fit people. Each box had a lid so one could close the box and be left in privacy or leave it open and communicate with others on the bus. I noticed quickly that a few Amoenians closed their seat boxes.

The strangest thing about the transport was that it didn't make much noise as it ran the way a bus or a train does. During the whole trip, all I could hear were the voices of the others on the transport rather than the transport itself. If you listened real closely, the loudest thing you could hear was a soft "cuuuush" sound, like the sound a coin makes when it's rolling on its side.

As we drove and stopped, different Amoenians got off the transport. Most had a bag of some sort, and I assumed they were going to work and their bag was like a briefcase. For the majority of the trip, I kept my eyes on the buildings on the side of the road. I had the window seat, and Sophia sat on the end. There was one type of building – a large square building made almost entirely of what looked like cement – that I kept seeing every few blocks throughout Amoena Vieta. And every one of these square buildings had the same emblem on them. On the top of every one was a circle containing each and every symbol of a major religion I could recognize. The only reason I knew all the symbols was due to that world religions course I took. On each one, there was a metal crucifix with a figure of Christ on it, and next to that was the Star and Crescent of Islam, the OM symbol of Hinduism, the Jade Emperor of the Chinese folk religion, the Buddhist Wheel of Life, the Khanda of Sikhism, the vine branch of Spiritism, Judaism's Star of David, the nine-pointed star of Baha'I, the Torii Gate of Shinto, the –

Every single one of the world's major religions was symbolized there in the circle of statues. Even the atomic whirl of *atheism* was symbolized.

All of the symbols were on top of every one of these buildings. They were illustrated through big circles and each of the circles displayed the same type of image that I saw on the capital building – two large hands shaking one another. The symbol represented the centerpiece that linked all the religions together. Sophia told me, "Humanity linked them all."

"What were the buildings, then? Churches?" I asked Sophia.

Sophia turned to me and replied,

"No, John, they're not churches. They are called community centers and they exist in every local peoplement throughout Amoena Vieta. You see, Amoenians recognize the necessity and importance of religion, and, at the same time, they see the countless and abhorrent atrocities that were committed in the name of God. To rectify the divisiveness that the world's major religions generated between brothers and sisters of the human family, The Council of Ecumenical Religiosity was formed by bringing together followers of the world's major religions. Again, the compromise was only made possible by the utilization of computers. By a systematic and democratic process, the peoples of the world stripped away the rituals and differences that excluded other religions. The Council sought to find the barebones, ecumenical doctrines that almost all religions taught, if any existed. The foundation of all major religions, they decided, rested on two principles: loving one another and loving God. And this is the understanding that most Amoenians have of religion – these are the major tenets that representatives from all major religions decided were the most crucial elements."

"Okay," I said. "So, what does that mean? How does religion work here, then?"

"Each religion is still practiced in Amoena Vieta: all the rituals, beliefs, and creeds native to each specific religion are freely practiced. No one can tell people what way to worship the God one believes in. It is part of the freedom of thought, the right to assemble, and the right to thine own self be true. There is, however, one burden that *is* placed on the religious individuals of Amoena Vieta. No religious doctrine can impede the Eternal Rights." Sophia's face became very serious, "No religious belief can serve as justification to *physically* diminish another religion's love for people or love for God: *whoever* they view God to be. In other words, while Amoenians can say whatever they want about another's religion, they are not allowed to forbid or deter anyone from partaking in their religious beliefs unless, of course, those religious beliefs contradict the Eternal Rights. This is the religious compromise borne of the Council of Ecumenical Religiosity. And that same council created the community centers you have seen in every town throughout our world. Inside their walls, all religious creeds are tolerated."

I couldn't believe it. How could anyone or anything get all those different religions under the same roof? I said with a little sarcasm in my voice, "Well, if all the people believe in different religions who are in those community centers, what, exactly, is it that they do in there?"

"It is a place where all major religions share the two most important principles: love of neighbor and love of God – whoever they view God to be. Amoenians from all over the local peoplement come together in the community centers to converse. Their goals, based on those two principles, are to figure out ways to make the community better by helping each other directly, or, as a way of pleasing their Creator. Everyone generally believes in the love of a neighbor. Only atheists abstain from pleasing their Creator because, of course, they do not believe one exists. Often the various elected local representatives listen to the people at the community centers so they can better represent the wishes of all of the people."

I was stunned. Again, it seemed so simple and so possible.

Now, you might think that there's no way to get all the religions in the world to be in unison like that. I didn't either, and so I said it to Sophia. But she only shook her head and told me I had little faith in the human family. She told me that in most instances if things are explained to human beings in reasonable terms and we appealed to the higher moral leanings of love and goodness, compromise and reconciliation could be the two-pronged ends of almost every dispute. She said that it is easy to forget this simple rule and that human beings, by their forgetful nature, will ceaselessly lose sight of it. The Amoenians began teaching the compromise and reconciliation approach to problem-solving early on in their schools. The Amoenian children repetitively digested this simple wisdom at an early age. Once the old approach of war to problem-solving was conditioned from the human psyche, all things became possible. In other words, the Amoenians realized that the solution to war was compromise and the way to cultivate compromise as a problem-solving method was to change the culture. Sophia said that the war instinct did not disappear entirely and most likely never will. But it does fade with education and through education's offspring: culture. She said that this is one way to approach all problems that are innate to human beings: through culture and education.

They applied the principle to religion and taught it young and early after the Council on Ecumenical Religiosity. Love of neighbor and love of God – this was what they found to be the fundamental truths of all religions, and it became the religious covenant between humanity in Amoena Vieta.

* * *

The transport slid softly to a halt in some wooded, hilly area – an area that looked like one of our state parks. The greenery was everywhere and it had a real peaceful atmosphere. That sweet sun seemed to cover every square inch of Amoena Vieta. Every square inch.

We – Sophia and me – got out when the transport stopped. I looked at the vegetation and let the serenity just sort of creep into me. I saw a narrow river not fifty feet from us, although I can never really estimate distances. The river made a calm, soothing sound that could put a baby to sleep and calmed me all the more. We started walking side by side down a little gravel path in front of the transport station. It was the same kind of road... it was so similar it might have even *been* the same road as the one in the capital. The only difference was that this section of the road was composed of gravel, while the section in the capital was composed of cobblestone.

While we walked, I was surrounded by a symphony of sounds similar to those in the capital, too. Children's laughter, dogs barking, people talking – the only thing that was different was the sound of the river and the number of people. There were a *lot* less people. It was then I realized we must be in the country, you know, in one of the local peoplements Sophia kept going on and on about.

So, I asked her. "Where'd you take me, Sophia?"

"I took you to see a local peoplement," she said in her usual calm, sage-like tone. "You have seen the global servicement. I want to show you an example of a local peoplement now."

"What *exactly* is it, anyway?"

"It is an arbitrary grouping of 700 households, based on location. The size of a local peoplement can change – but that is something that is left to the global servicement because it is mandated for all local peoplements."

"Mandated? Why?"

"Because the size of the local peoplements is one of the key facets of Amoena Vieta. We have found that the easiest and most efficient way to ensure that a peoplement serves the people lies in its population. The fewer people the servicement has to deliver services to, the more efficient and equitable the job. Think of it on a microcosmic level. Is it easier for a teacher to effectively teach fifteen or one hundred students?"

"Obviously fifteen," I answered without hesitation.

"Why?"

"Well... because there's less chaos – fewer students for the teacher to, well, teach."

"We agree. That is why every local peoplement must be composed of a certain number of individuals – to ensure the peoplement can properly service the people. People can travel anywhere in the world, but their civic duty remains to the local peoplement in which they are a resident. And the small size of a peoplement has an endless number of positive effects. That is why it is the foundation of our city structure. Smaller places are more *manageable* places. For instance, in a city of merely 700 households, a sense of community – of wholeness – a *true* humanitarian feeling amongst the residents can be cultivated and where each vote – each person – *truly* feels they have a role. The population philosophy simplifies virtually all aspects of the community and magnifies the peoplement's ability to serve *all* the people."

"But then, aren't there just factions that form? What I mean is... aren't some local peoplements primarily made of a certain group which dominates the other groups?"

A cool breeze came over our bodies as Sophia replied, "That is a good question. There will always be factions and people who try to claim superiority for this reason or that amongst any people. The quest for feeling superior never strays too far from the human heart. But the Amoeanian emphasis on education and their pervading philosophy of humanism keep these factions at a minimum.

"Also, the sizes of the factions usually tend to be small. Every local peoplement is always drawn to be kept under 1,000 people. But the current global mandate is that a local peoplement must be composed of 700 households. That also makes all services delivered to the population a manageable task."

"Okay. But if a local peoplement is made up of 700 households, and there are, say, ten billion people on the earth, aren't there a ridiculous amount of local peoplements?"

She smiled as she spoke, "Sure, John. There are many local peoplements in which every single person plays a role and every person matters."

I thought a minute before I realized, "You're right. I see what you mean. Where I'm from, we divide our country into states, our states into counties, and our counties into municipalities. Municipalities are the smallest: there must be a million of them. I guess it's pretty similar to your local peoplement. But are peoplements self-sufficient?"

"Nothing is entirely self-sufficient. But peoplements do strive to be so. If they are unable, due to a wide variety of reasons such as the lack of the natural resources needed to be self-sufficient, the global servicement redistributes a little of the wealth to make them relatively self-sufficient."

"I think I understand," I said. But I didn't, really. It took me until later to see actually what she meant.

It was then I thought I saw a contradiction in what she said and tried to call her out on it. "Where we just were – the capital – wasn't that a local peoplement, too?"

"Yes," Sophia said like a teacher who was surprised her student knew the answer to some difficult question, "Where we were was composed entirely of local peoplements."

"But look," I wagged my arm back and forth at the lack of people on and around the path, "There are so fewer people where we are now, aren't there? How can it be, then, that both places are local peoplements with the same amount of population? It makes no sense, Sophia. I can see there are fewer people here than where we just were before!"

Sophia laughed. Her bright white teeth and beautifully shaped oval face couldn't help but make me smile. "The density of population is irrelevant to the composition of local peoplements. As I said, the current global rule is that local peoplements are composed of 700 households. This can change but cannot exceed 1,000 people. It does not matter at all if each of the 700 households are right next to each other in apartment buildings or several hundred meters apart – the fact is that every 700 households compose each local peoplement. Put simply, twenty local peoplements can be right next to each other and live in one densely populated area – like in the global capital where we just were."

I thought for a moment. How are people supposed to be able to move when they're obligated to function in a specific local peoplement? I mean, when people move around – which they naturally do – there is no way a local peoplement can exist as Sophia defines it! People don't just remain in one place their whole lives... it's not possible and can be undesirable for some. If people don't stay in their local peoplement, then each local peoplement cannot be truly representative of the whole population.

But then I asked Sophia. And, as always, she had an answer.

"The local peoplements *can* retain representativeness of the whole *while* maintaining the specific number required for each local peoplement. A local peoplement is not a caste or a segregated group. Amoenians need only fill out applications and find availability in another place in order to move from one local peoplement to another."

She said it's not very different from the way we do it now. If you want to move into a community, you must wait for a house or apartment to become available. It's the same basic idea, really. I was like you – I didn't get it at all at first. But the more I thought about it, the more sense it made.

But I thought about this and the restrictive nature of it. I wondered, "Couldn't you just go where you wanted?" I turned and asked Sophia.

Sophia responded in her soft, kind voice, "You could go anywhere anytime you please. *Traveling* to a different local peoplement is much different from being *part* of a different local peoplement."

I was really taken aback by all the freedom. Sophia said that *any* Amoenian could travel any-where they pleased virtually anytime. They need only to continue to perform their duties to the local peoplement of where they are a member. So, you see – anyone can travel anywhere. It's just a matter of ensuring they have their computer with them and stay up to date on the duties that a democracy demands, you know?

Sophia then explained the entire concept of local peoplements and their necessity for the common good. She said that local peoplements make people feel a "nascent need for national-ism" beyond their fealty to Amoena Vieta. This urge toward nationalism, she said, was inherent to human nature and has been since the first nations. The problem for Amoenian society was finding a way not to allow the divisiveness of nationalism to allow sects to form amongst the human family and result in countless wars between brothers and sisters. Sophia said that belonging to a certain local peoplement, is another Amoenian way that serves to vent this basic human need for nationalism, which she emphasized is a natural but often problematic instinct. Local peoplements provide an outlet for any excess nationalism that human beings have. The global servicement ensures that the local peoplements are never enabled to break off or fight with other local peoplements. And, of course, the people, as a whole, regulate and control the global servicement – making sure it never gets too high and mighty in its role as a peacekeeper. The people control how much power the global servicemen has at all times by controlling the resources it is allowed to have at all times. And Sophia told me that the other major reason – the more important reason – that Amoenians created local peoplements was in order to make the community more accessible and, by default, more beholden to its citizenry. In other words, in the peoplements, each person has a good deal of influence. In every peoplement, she said, every person knows that they truly *count*. That, as Sophia told me, is far more humane *and* efficient at serving the needs of the people as they know that their voice is being heard.

As we walked, I saw many different animals. The setting was different in the local peoplement – even more, I guess you could say, beautiful to me. Insects and deer, different kinds of dogs and cats, rabbits, and what looked like caribou were just a few of the animals I saw cross the gravel path that we walked together.

"Why is everything so different, Sophia? I mean, the wildlife and the atmosphere. Why is it so much… better?"

"Some Amoenians like to be in a crowded area, people living on top of and below them, with constant action and excitement all around. Others prefer sparseness, and the blessed touch of nature, trees, animals, and a slow, more meditative, peaceful existence. Both are available to all Amoenians. It is like your idea of the differences between city and country life. Both are preserved here in Amoena Vieta. Either can be attained by any Amoenian, depending on personal preference and other factors."

We continued along the path, and I couldn't help but notice our passing of a constant chain of buildings that did not have the same distinction as the houses – these buildings were different: they had statues of strange symbols on them. Every so often along the string of houses, I would see these different structures with signs in the front with text I could not understand written on them.

"What are they?" I asked as my curiosity peaked.

"Most of the buildings with the statues and the signs are essentially what you know as small businesses and others are community aid houses. Small businesses are generally places that Amoenians set up when they believe they can produce a product the general populous desires. But be patient, John. I will explain it all to you," she said as we continued our pace forward. Every so often, the wind would blow and bless our faces with the cool air from some torrent.

I studied the small businesses and community aid houses we were passing every so often on the path. I watched people enter and leave and it was as if some of the buildings had a revolving door out front. But I did not bring it up again so as not to annoy my mentor. And she did get to it, just as promised. It was only a matter of time – when Sophia said she was going to do something, you could count on it.

* * *

We came up to a local peoplement building in no time. It was just like the global servicement capital she took me to – the same basic setup. The building appeared to be just like all the others around it, but, once inside, I could see it was far deeper than the other buildings in the local peoplement. A large marble tablet with the Amoenian Eternal Rights was nailed to the front door. The white building was rectangular and there was the same statue of two big marble hands shaking each other jutting out from the top of the building, sort of like they were the flower, and the building was the root of a great plant.

It may sound exactly the same, but it wasn't. I noticed some differences – it wasn't an exact replica. For instance, the marble had a nicer shine and the hands on top of the building were bigger, and I noticed the Eternal Rights were carved into a different kind of stone on the local peoplement building than the one on the global servicement building. And it was greener there than in the global capital – not much – but still greener. Little things like that – superficial stuff – were different. But for the most part, the local peoplement capital building was a spot-on match.

We went on through the metal door and into the building. The first thing that struck me was a… a scent, sort of like freshly brewed coffee. It wasn't exactly like that, but it was a pleasant smell. Everything else inside was similar to the inside of the global capital, too – just scaled down – much smaller. There were a bunch of Amoenians sitting in a giant circle. Everyone was dressed in different clothes – casual sort of clothes. This time, I noticed the big screens hanging from the ceiling before I even sat down. There were only two screens instead of four and they looked the same as the screens in the global capital, only smaller and with less text.

Amidst the constant chorus of voices that reigned throughout the local peoplement building, Sophia led me to a plush purple seat on the edge of the circle. I looked around and saw a sea of laptops on the laps of everyone, just like in the global capital. In the middle of the circle, underneath the screens, a small group of individuals sat clustered together, apart from the mass of people who encircled them. The seven individuals in the center spoke, wrote, and looked at their laptops, just like all the other Amoenians who surrounded them.

After I took in the view and noticed how similar everything was to the global capital, I spoke up,

"It's a lot like a little replica of the global capital."

Sophia shook her head. "No, you have it backwards. The global capital is the replica of the local capital. The global capital needs only be larger because it affects everyone and, therefore, must accommodate everyone. But larger does not connote better in Amoena Vieta. You mustn't make that mistake. Less is more. The Amoenians saw the necessity to design a system of servicement in a world with billions of people in which the individual did not get lost in the herd while, at the same time, the system had to uphold the ultimate, beautiful, familial ideal in which collectivism is rooted. Little peoplements, overseen by a global servicement, enabled us to strike that necessary balance. In a community composed of a maximum of 700 households, *every* person's voice becomes essential. That is the reason we made local peoplements consist of a set number of individuals: to preserve the all-important human longing for a unique, personal identity and individuality. It is easier to be counted and to count when you are one in seven hundred rather than one in seven billion. It is remarkably easy to get the individual to pay attention to the good of the whole when they know that their civic duty is significant and meaningful. Less is more, John. Less is more."

"Does this work the same way, though?" I asked, "I mean... the large screens and the laptop and the circular design all look so similar... is the process, too?"

"The servicement setup is similar in local peoplements. It hinges on the same basic principles as global servicements. Local peoplements have a parliamentary system composed of elected representatives and the peoplement. Only here the roles are reversed. The people – the 700 households in every local peoplement – can vote *directly* on the local peoplement's laws. The seven representatives you see in the middle of the circle are elected by the people in the local peoplement," Sophia said and pointed her arm with its soft, bronze skin toward the group of seven individuals seated in the space in the middle of all the chairs. "They draw up the laws and measures of the local peoplement based on the desires of their constituents. They also are given the veto power in local peoplements. The seven local representatives – one for every hundred people – use their knowledge to determine how much extra of a *local* minimum – the amount of a good and service that every person must be given *above* the global minimum that can be supplied to all the residents of the local peoplement. That is their power – given to them by the people who elected them. They must decide if the people's desires to create a higher local minimum are feasible given the resources and labor power of the local peoplement. Then, they can veto the people's desires if they deem them unreasonable. They also serve as the tiebreaker's vote if the people split on an issue, 350-350."

"What about the global representatives? Where are they?"

"They are orchestrating the oversight groups necessary in each local peoplement. They continually ensure that the *global* minimum is being supplied – amongst their other responsibilities. Suppose a local peoplement decided that they can produce more of a global minimum – and create a higher, local minimum. In that case, the global representatives are also in charge of ensuring that a new local minimum is being observed. The global representatives have other responsibilities as I have discussed. They are primarily overseers – checks and balances on the local peoplements."

I nodded and then thought for a moment. "I see. So, the global representatives are sort of out of this picture. But what about if the seven local representatives get out of control? It seems they get quite a bit of power – being able to veto the people and all. What happens then?"

Sophia answered without even momentary hesitation. "Then the people throw out the abusive local representative and elect a new one. The Amoenians did away with erroneous 'fixed' terms that only served to make the representative beholden to people until election time. As soon as the representatives stop serving the electors, the electors can, by majority vote, abdicate the representatives," she said, and I watched a wry smile come upon her face, "It is a constant and steady political diet of a *true* and feasible democracy that pumps throughout Amoena Vieta. Because how else can a commonweal, truly beholden to the people and for the good of the masses, be run other than by the beauty of democracy?"

At that moment, I thought I saw a gaping hole in the fabric of their society. I pounced on the perceived flaw like a hungry cat. I think I was so eager to find a flaw, partly in defense of my own system and partly as a personal defense mechanism. I just didn't know how our society could have missed some of these things that are so simple, and yet make society so much better, you know? So, I tried to fool her.

"Amoena Vieta is a democracy, as you say, and a democracy is, by definition, only beholden to the majority, right, Sophia?"

She immediately nodded, "Yes, John."

"But a true commonwealth – or commonweal as you've called it – is beholden to *all* the people, right?" I was grinning as I spoke because I was sure I had her.

"Of course. A commonweal could not be a *common* weal unless it served the good of *all* people. But John –"

"Well, if a democracy only serves the majority, and a commonwealth serves everyone, how, then, can Amoena Vieta call itself *both* a commonwealth *and* a democracy?" My smile was spread from ear to ear as I asked the question. But to my surprise, Sophia did not look confused or bewildered in any way. She didn't make a strange, unknowing face or even hesitate more than a moment before responding. It was as if she expected the question all along.

"You make a very good and valid point. Our philosophers grappled with this point before the founding of Amoena Vieta. Of course, the ultimate remedy to the problem of majority or mass rule is for everyone to be a part of the majority – which is a contradiction in terms. But almighty individuality cannot be preserved in a state that is solely based on majority rule – the majority consumes the individual. So, a true commonweal *must* be devoted to the individual just as it is devoted to the group," she said as she looked deeply and seriously into my eyes. "The price of majority rule is the marginalization of small factions that form amongst the people. Small factions and unique individuals are generally the losers in a democratic system. To circumvent this unfortunate fact, the Amoenians have instituted a safety net that runs underneath the fabric of our democratic society. We have designed a metaphorical fishnet laid at the bottom of our societal floor that is inescapable and always there to lift all those who fall into it due to their individuality or uniqueness. The Eternal Rights are the basis of this metaphorical fishnet. As I said before, those rights serve to protect the individual liberties that enable individuals to be just that – individuals, their right to speak and act any way they choose so long as it does not directly hurt another. It is easy to see that Eternal Rights serve as the basis of social liberty and preserve the social liberty that makes individuals unique. And the Eternal Rights also serve as a fish-net for the economic liberty that is also necessary to preserve the uniqueness of the individual. I will tell you much more about this aspect of our safety net when I show you our economy. Suffice to say that the Eternal Rights are what enabled Amoena Vieta to balance between democratic majority rule with individualism and minority rights. Our society is structured in such a way as to include all members of the great human family. Because being a member of the human family necessitates concern and love for all its family members. I need not tell a Christian man such as you the wisdom of this sentiment," she said, as she motioned to the chain with the crucifix that I had hanging around my neck. "You know full well the familial view of humanity runs throughout the New Testament of your religion," Sophia said before trailing off, looking at the screen at the top of the room. Her thin dark eyebrows furrowed, and an entirely new and even more serene and beautiful expression washed over her face. "Do you have any other questions about our local peoplement, John?" she asked, and her bronze arm swept the air as if she were redirecting my concentration toward the screen in the middle of the room.

The most obvious question I could think of was the first to conjure itself in my mind. "Yeah, sure I do. How do Amoenians find the time to do all this voting, vetoing, and what not? I saw the little businesses as we walked on the path before, and I saw inside the windows that the people were busy working. How can they find the time to do all this voting when they're working and taking care of their kids?"

Sophia sat back in her plush purple seat and turned towards me. Her eyes remained focused on mine as she spoke, "Amoenians are conscious of their economy of time. That is why civil duties to the local peoplements are similar to those of the global servicements. It takes a mere week annually to vote on all the measures and laws passed in the global servicement every year and three years to pass all the measures and laws on the local peoplement. The seven elected local peoplement representatives spend the vast majority of their time, like the global representatives, enforcing the minimums that were passed and composing pre-laws – what you call bills – upon the people's suggestions. Pre-laws require a certain measure of what you call 'grassroots' support, and once that is gotten, the seven representatives are responsible for composing the supported pre-laws into presentable and easily comprehensible documents. Each pre-law is then broken down and summarized for the people by the representative as well as the media and any other groups who choose to outline the pre-law. The outlined pre-laws are then voted on in the three weeks cycle each year by the seven hundred individuals who compose each local peoplement. All pre-laws composed throughout the year by the seven representatives are voted on within those three weeks."

"Everyone votes in the local peoplement, too? It is mandatory like for the global servicement?"

"Of course. Voting is not optional to anyone in the commonweal. The only exemptions are the youth – those who have not completed their education and those who cannot vote due to mental or physical incapacitation," Sophia said adamantly. "Voting is one of the few things that are compulsory in Amoena Vieta, and it is only mandatory because it is absolutely *essential* for the function of a true commonweal that *everyone* votes. Every educated voice must be heard for the servicement to serve everyone. Ergo, voting is a legal obligation."

I looked at her confusedly. "You mean it's actually *against* Amoenian law not to vote?"

"Yes," she replied immediately. "It is the *only* way to ensure the common good is actually the *common* good. It is the only way to ensure that the servicement serves the people – *all* the people. It is one of the only restrictions on the Eternal Right of self-expression. Everyone *must* participate so that society truly serves everyone."

The confused look remained on my face. I mean, it seemed harsh to make people vote, and it seemed to me that obligatory voting was against the Eternal Right to self-expression. Sophia picked up on my concern as if she were reading my mind.

"Don't be surprised. Obligatory voting is not a strange or unreasonable concept. It is strikingly similar to a concept you are used to."

"What do you mean?"

"Is everyone obligated to pay taxes in your country?"

"Yes."

"Why? What is the reason for mandatory tax payments?"

"Well," I said as for the first time I actually considered *why* I paid taxes, "because services cost money. Because everyone needs to chip some of their monetary resources to, you know, make services work."

"Then you understand our reason, *everyone* must chip in material goods – money – for society to function. So then, how is it any different with ideas and worldviews? Doesn't everyone also have an obligation to put in their thoughts for a society to work well and serve everyone?"

"Well," I said, inhaling a deep breath of the coffee-smelling air that permeated the local peoplement, "I guess I never really thought about it that way."

"Think about this then. If the whole of society is obligated to put some of their material wealth into society for it to function, but only *some* of the people put their ideas – their intellectual wealth into society, do you believe the material wealth that everyone puts in will be used for the good of all that society? Or is it more likely that the material wealth put in by all will be distributed primarily amongst those individuals of that society who choose to decide where that wealth will go? In other words, those who vote control a democratic society. Therefore, those who vote determine the material distribution of that society. Since human beings are naturally self-interested, those who vote usually vote to enrich themselves before they vote to enrich others. Obligatory voting eliminates that flaw in most previous democracies. Do you understand, John?"

"It depends on the people who vote, though, Sophia. It depends whether the part of society who does vote believes the wealth should be spread across society or whether it should be funneled to themselves," I said. It was then I realized the implication of what she was saying. "It seems to me that you don't have a lot of faith in people if you don't mind my saying so. If you did, you would trust any segment of the population to vote in such a way as to spread the wealth across the population."

Sophia instantly laughed a soft, sweet, angelic little chuckle. "Oh no, John! That's not it at all. Most Amoenians have a great deal of faith in the goodness of humankind. It's just that we live in a world that is at least largely made of material – of tangible reality. The Capitalist economic system that was such a part of the old world was drenched with the idea that one should acquire as much tangible reality or 'things' for oneself as possible. In other words, the human vice of greed not only fuels but forms the bedrock of Capitalist societies. The economic system of a society can't help but influence all other aspects of that society. Therefore, the democratic political systems of Capitalist societies serve as a reflection of the ideology of greed. The people in these societies generally vote to bolster their own economic status – fulfilling the Capitalist ideology drummed into them since birth. The result was widespread economic inequality – those who didn't vote had little, while those who did vote had lots. This economic polarization due to uneven participation of voting causes social polarization." She paused and squinted at for a moment before continuing, "The way to eliminate this parasite on the back of the commonweal was to make it obligatory for *all* to vote."

"Wait," I interrupted. "You say it is from the economic system that the societal domino effect occurs. Why not just change the economic system then?"

"Because the problem will occur virtually in any economic system. Capitalism places wealth in the hands of the 'fittest' and lends itself to an ideology of greed. Its antithesis, Communism, disperses the wealth more evenly but unevenly distributes the *power* in society, which is also very dangerous. Democratism places the power in the people's hands, and with that power, they may do what they please – but they must do it as a *whole*. But for Democratism to work, everyone must vote. Democratism's ideology rests on inclusion rather than on greed or power. Everyone must vote so that the majority can have what they want and the minority will still have their needs satisfied by the Eternal Rights," she brushed her black hair back with both hands before continuing, "So you see, in order for a society to serve the needs of all its members, all the members of a society must vote: only then can it be a society of, by, and for the *people*. The invention of the computer gave us not only the capability to ensure that everyone votes, but also the capability to vote easily. It is not a difficult concept. Everyone must vote in Amoena Vieta; everyone must put some of both their material wealth *and* their intellectual wealth into the society for the society to serve all."

* * *

The only aspect I wasn't sure about was the whole computer thing. I've never known a computer that couldn't be hacked. So, I asked Sophia,

"At the core of the Democratist economic system is democracy. And democracy in Amoena Vieta depends on computers and the internet. But how can you trust the computer? What I mean is everything you say *sounds* good and all, but it all hinges on computers being flawless – and computers are not flawless. People can, you know, hack them…"

Sophia brushed another few strands of dark hair away from her face and around her ear.

"Computers in your land will be made 100% secure before very long. Technology is right around the corner. And their use will be taught early and often in your educational system, as in ours. Computers will become the material entity that links us all. Most Amoenians believe we are already all linked in spirit. The computer: the internet, to be more specific, fills the void between spirit and tangible reality. And we have made them very safe as voting machines. That is all you can ask for. Some level of trust is always required between people."

I nodded.

"Most voting in Amoena Vieta is done solely via the internet – all the people's vetoes, for instance. But the most important votes – minimums, office removal, and representative elections – are not done by computer alone. These aspects of global servicement and local peoplements are submitted via the internet. But a paper receipt is printed as well. Each local peoplement is responsible for ensuring they have seven hundred voting receipts for these major aspects of both servicements. A global and a local committee is appointed from amongst the people to ensure the legitimacy of the process, and the rest of the population in each local peoplement are freely allowed to count the anonymous votes themselves to ensure their local peoplement's tabulation is accurate. We have designed a system where there is virtually no uncertainty as to the true outcome of the vote – it can be checked and rechecked by any person in each local peoplement. The people of each local peoplement can communicate with other local peoplements via the internet to ensure the global vote is also accurate. Everything is traceable in our democratic system: records are kept for both local and global voting. But as always, in anything human, *some* trust is required for it to work. Anything that is made and conducted by human beings requires some degree of trust in human beings. That is unavoidable."

What she said made sense, and I was satisfied with the answer to my question. I could understand that computers would be virtually fool-proof secure in the years to come, and even if they were never 100% secure – it is good enough, you know? So, I moved on to what I thought was the next logical question,

"I think I understand how votes are cast and counted. But you haven't explained to me who actually serves the people. What I mean is, how are candidates picked to run?" I asked, and as I spoke, my eyes drifted over to a diminutive man with small, beady eyes. He sat before a laptop in the local servicement room and furrowed his eyebrows as he angrily slammed the keys. His gimlet eyes gazed up in radiating anger at the screen above him. A stream of what to me sounded like a scream in gibberish immediately began spewing from his furious mouth. The little man's fist began shaking repeatedly toward the screen. I watched as some of the bronze figures around him looked over with what seemed like disdain and disapproval on their faces. The diminutive man did not stop his fist shaking or the stream of anger. Then a sweet, cherub-faced woman who sat in front of the man turned around. I watched her blue eyes closely as they looked the man over. Before long, she raised her hand out to him – palm open – and said, "Lo okay, hermano, lo okay." Then, she patted him on the shoulder twice and turned back around. It wasn't long before the man hushed like a baby who'd received a pacifier.

It was then that I realized Sophia had been speaking the whole time while I was entranced by the angry man and calming woman. I embarrassingly interrupted,

"I'm sorry, Sophia. Could you start again? I kind of drifted off during the explanation, what with all the new sights and sounds I'm taking in."

"Of course, John," she said with a relieving mix of patience and understanding, "As you know, our voting system is double-tiered – there are local and global elections. Each is held during the weeks of the year dedicated to voting so that voters can focus on each election as it comes and not be overwhelmed by politics all at once. They do not occur at the same time, but I am showing you both on the same day so that you may understand our system. The two elections – while both democratic – are very different in nature. Which would you like to hear about first?"

"Local peoplement," I said without hesitation. It seemed natural to start with the more important one and go on to the less important one.

"Okay. For every local election, there are seven hundred prospective households – anyone and everyone can offer to serve the people. We use a system of voluntary participation in local peoplements so that everyone who is willing to run for representative truly has a chance. There is no *unitrade* – or money – involved in our election process preventing the wealthy or the well-connected participant from disproportionate influence. It is money that lurks at the heart of the corruption of all democracies. We have removed that possibility from occurring in Amoena Vieta.

"About a month before the local elections, each willing candidate of the seven hundred composes an *ideosheet* and submits it to the elections board – a group that is appointed by one of the local peoplement's officials each year. An ideosheet is a candidate's resume and philosophy. It lists where they stand on each issue. Each candidate describes why they believe they are the best person for that particular position and lists a succinct version of their political ideology. The ideology each candidate has is their own and can be as varying as can the human imagination: with the only exception being that none of the ideologies can impede the Eternal Rights. There are liberals, Marxists, conservatives, fascists, oligarchists, monarchists, and every other conceivable political philosophy listed by candidates in each election. Wherein these political philosophies contradict the Eternal Rights, they are edited to be adaptable. For instance, a fascist could not run on the platform of eliminating the right to education since that is one of the Eternal Rights. Eternal Rights cannot be denied by any local peoplement – this is a global law and, as I said, the foundation of the protection of the minority in a democracy. A fascist could, however, run on the premise that some were entitled to a higher or more advanced education than the basic education that the Eternal Rights entitle to all people. A change in the Eternal Rights can only be done via a super-majority vote – 98% of the populous – which, needless to say, is nearly impossible to achieve. No one local peoplement can change an Eternal Right, and so, no candidate running as a fascist can run on a position that denies the Eternal Rights of the people. Incidentally, in the centuries that Amoena Vieta has existed, there has never been a fascist elected in any local peoplement. Do you understand?"

"Sure," I said as I glanced up at one of the screens above. "All political philosophies can be advocated by local peoplement candidates insofar as their platform does not impede the Eternal Rights of the people, since the Eternal Rights are universally guaranteed by human law.

"What I don't understand is why no fascist has ever been elected. I mean, if there is freedom of thought and self-expression, knowing the diversity of beliefs people have, why has a fascist never been successful in any local peoplement?"

"In one word: education," she said and smiled. "The Amoenians understand that a well-functioning democracy necessitates that the voters be well educated. Therefore, the highest emphasis in Amoena Vieta is placed on the education of the members of our society: that is one of the reasons why the right to an education is considered an Eternal Right here. With education also comes compassion and love for others – two of the fundamental pillars of a good society. We feel they are the most important and essential human qualities. With compassion and love for others comes the general elimination of certain political philosophies that are devoid of compassion –"

"Like fascism," I interjected.

"Exactly. An educated populace will almost never choose fascism – the two are enemies in the goodness of the human heart. Educated individuals are, more often than not, more compassionate individuals. It is one of our proofs of the goodness of humankind – that with more understanding of the world comes more compassion toward others. Do you see, John?" she asked before quickly glancing at the telescreen and looking back at me.

"Sure, I see."

"Okay. Then I will continue describing the local peoplement election process. Once all the candidates submit their ideosheet, the board of elections is responsible for compiling a set of ideosheets containing all the beliefs, stances on issues, and philosophical bases of each candidate running in the local peoplement. The board of elections then disperses an ideosheet for each candidate to all 700 households. The process is easy and simple."

"Sure," I said, "but how can you ensure the fairness of the board of elections? It seems that their honesty is central to the whole process thus far."

Sophia answered without hesitation. "The local media scrutinizes all electoral processes to the point where any kind of corruption is almost impossible. And the people: the keystone of Amoena Vieta, constantly keep an eye on the media, as I will show you later. It is not difficult to provide functioning checks and balances on every system in society when the society is manageable by being scaled down to a mere 700 households. When democracies are reduced to functional sizes in which everyone has at least heard of everyone else and when everyone is made to take part in the functioning of servicement or peoplement, a democracy is remarkably difficult to corrupt. The size of local peoplements and the participation of all members ensure the functionality of the commonweal."

"Okay," I nodded, "so the ideosheets are dispersed a month in advance to be scrutinized by the voters before the election. Then what?"

"The people take a month to weed out the candidates whose ideas they disagree with and to select those whose ideas they agree with. Each candidate's ideosheet is about one page long, and it takes remarkably little time and effort for most of our educated populace to decide who they do and don't want to serve them. During the month before elections, the populace can freely ask questions of the candidates in whom they are interested. The candidates have a legal obligation to be accessible to the people. That is part of the agreement when they throw their hat in the ring. The represented must be extremely available to the representees."

"Okay, but wait a second," I interrupted before my eyes momentarily wandered over to the little man. He was calm and complacent and smiling at the screen now. I concluded that the next legislative measure must have gone the way he hoped it would. I looked at Sophia and continued, "You said that the people, and not the representatives, were the ones with the power in the local peoplement, too. Why all the trouble over the representatives, then? It is more like a direct democracy – so why waste all this time on ideosheets and representatives?"

"The people do have the power, John. They pass all the local peoplement's laws for a year in those three weeks. But as I said before, the representative has the power to put forth the measures that will be voted on in those three weeks. That is a great power, John. And, as all powers in the peoplement, they are derived from the people."

I laughed, "But that's *all* the local peoplement's representatives do? Put forth agendas and codify laws and assess local minimums?"

"No. As I said, they are also in charge of coordinating the groups in the local peoplement who serve as checks on the various systems in the local peoplement. Therefore, they have the power of appointment. As you know, one of the foundations of Amoena Vieta is that every power has a check and a balance, with exception to the power of the people as a whole. The checks on all societal institutions are monitored by appointment commissions. Each representative has the obligation and power to appoint the individuals in the commonweal who will preside over each commission. Those five powers – bill formation, local minimum assessment, agenda setting, commission appointment, and watchdog coordination are the solemn duties of the local peoplement representatives."

It seemed simple enough. "I see. And seven of the seven hundred households in each local peoplement are elected as representatives for the local peoplement, right?"

"Yes."

"Okay. Now, how many people are in these watchdog commissions you're talking about?"

"The rest," Sophia said with a serious face.

My jaw dropped in shock.

"The rest? You mean everyone left outside of these seven people is in watchdog commissions?"

"No, not quite. I misspoke. There is also a global representative who coordinates the global watchdog commissions. Everyone else is in watchdog commissions in each local peoplement – some are doing oversight for the local peoplement minimums and laws, others are doing oversight for the global minimums.

"Conducting oversight, along with voting and performing legal duties, are amongst the major civic responsibilities. Every functional person over a certain age must be a part of a commission to oversee some institution in the commonwealth. The representatives are responsible for the committees they appoint. If an institution being overseen – like a global minimum making group, for instance – is not being watched effectively by the committee appointed to do so, the representative who appointed the committee – and the committee – may be removed by vote and replaced," she paused and smiled. "There are no elected untouchables, John – that is the road to tyranny. A representative can be replaced at any time. That keeps the representative in service of the people."

"It seems that being a representative is a tough job, Sophia. What do they get for serving?"

"You are right to say it is a tough job. In fact, it is easily the hardest job there is in terms of responsibility, John. It is the job of serving the people. But that makes it the most fulfilling as well. It ought to be the toughest job. And in terms of satisfaction, it receives the noblest and most sought-after reward there is – the contentment of helping people and making their lives better," she said before pausing. Her eyes looked at me with a sort of sweet, loving look before continuing, "But if you are asking what level of unitrade the people are rewarded, since the Capitalist ideology you have been reared under preaches material compensation as the primary satisfaction one can receive from labor – the answer is that our representatives receive the median income. The representatives also have as ample a supply of necessities as does any Amoenian. The representatives get only a modicum of extra unitrade for their duties. This ensures that their motives are kept pure. What does it say about a representative's incentives if they are paid exorbitant amounts of material goods? The Amoenians have learned from the past. They saw the destruction and corruption of countless democracies due to the greed that is cultivated in an environment where the lust for money and power comes to exceed the lust for the welfare of the people."

"They get paid *nothing* extra?" I asked in astonishment. "But then why would anyone do it?"

"For the *right* reasons. To serve for the love of people more than the love of self. These are the motives a great representative of the people must have. Skill and intelligence are important in our representatives but are secondary to proper motivation. The Amoenians devised a system to weed out those with impure, materialistic, selfish motivations." She

paused thoughtfully for a moment and then continued, "You are a Christian, John. To put it in New
Testament terms you are likely familiar with, how
can someone serve by God and money?"

I nodded.

"Well, most Amoenians, Christian or not, understand that reasoning is particularly applicable to representatives of the people. How can a representative
serve the people while serving his or her own material desires? It is very difficult to do both effectively:
the human temptation of greed usually becomes too
tempting, and they end up serving themselves before
the people. Therefore, a true representative of the
people must be devoted to the people and not to her
or himself. That is the basis for why the Amoenians
saw the necessity of keeping the representatives
materially humble. This practice also ensures that
the representatives never allow global minimums
to fall too low – because that is primarily what will
sustain them. In order for representatives to advance
economically, the whole of society has to advance
economically. Our system *forces* the representative to
make self-interest the same as community interest.
And we have found it has produced far more selfless
representatives of the commonwealth: true representatives of the people," she said and then got up
out of the purple seat she was sat in. "Come on John,
you have a sense of the way our local peoplement's

work. You can continue to ask me questions as we go to our next destination."

I got up and began following Sophia towards the door of the local peoplement. "I think I understand. It is very interesting, Sophia. A lot to take in at once, though, you know?"

Sophia laughed softly, "I know John. It's a lot for anyone to take in at once. Even if you don't understand or remember it all, what you can remember may help."

Confusion struck me. "Huh? Help who?"

But Sophia did not reply. She made her way through a small crowd of people near the door and turned back to motion for me to follow.

"Follow me."

I followed obediently and felt like a kid going to open Christmas presents.

* * *

Sophia began walking back the way we had come. The sweet-smelling coffee scent of the local peoplement's building was quickly replaced by a pine-needle smell that hovered throughout the local peoplement we were in. I jogged towards Sophia and caught up with her in no time.

"Wait," I said, puffing in exhaustion from the short sprint, "I have more questions about the servicement."

Sophia smirked, and I went on, "What about the global servicement – you didn't tell me much about that other than their basic responsibilities of global minimums. How are they chosen? What else do they do?"

"I am delighted by your curiosity. The global servicement functions on the same keystone philosophy that Amoenians, for the most part, share. It is run by checks and balances, compassion for all beings, adherence to the Eternal Rights, and, above all, the people's will."

"Okay. But those are just broad principles. What exactly do they *do*? I mean, all the laws seem to be made by local peoplements, right?" I asked impatiently. I think she noticed my budding impatience, but didn't say anything about it.

"No. Not all laws are not made by local peoplements. Only most."

"Then what, again, does the global servicement do besides setting and monitoring global minimums? And how are they elected?"

She took a deep breath and began, "The global servicement representatives are elected in a similar way to the local representatives. The sole difference is that there is a prerequisite for the global servicement, whereas there is no prerequisite for the local peoplement. The prerequisite is not money or fame: it is experience. A global servicement official is chosen from the pool of local servicement representatives from all over Amoena Vieta. Those representatives who want to run must submit a declaration of candidacy and their views to a *global* servicement board, which is also chosen from the local peoplements. The global board composes ideosheets, and each person in Amoena Vieta is given one. Then comes the computer- run election..."

As Sophia spoke, we approached the transport station.

"Okay. But what does the global servicement *do*? What laws do they make?"

Sophia spoke as we boarded the transport. There was a large group of Amoenians boarding it, so I heard the chatter of voices on all sides. Sophia spoke directly into my ear as we sat side by side on the transport.

"The global servicement, as I said before, functions primarily to monitor and enforce global minimums and ensure that Eternal Rights are being observed. However, they also serve as a check on the local peoplements: they are one of the entities that the people may petition if they feel they are being dealt with unjustly by their local peoplements. The global representatives are in charge of assigning commissioners to oversee all aspects of whatever local peoplement they are given authority to watch. Suppose the global representative of a local peoplement does not ensure the allotted global minimum distribution. In that case, they may be immediately removed from office by the majority of the vote," she said and paused before continuing, "Again, John, there are no terms of time. Only competence and efficacy are valued. And, of course, the people always have the power to veto anything the global representative does. The representative has no power that the people cannot override.

"The global representative is elected in a similar span – except it needs less attention and is completed in one week. Once elected, they can be removed at any time and replaced by one of the current local peoplement representatives, or, in some cases, they choose a past representative."

"Okay," I said. "I think I understand. You still haven't explained the laws, though. What laws does the global servicement make?"

Sophia pushed a few strands of her dark hair out of her face and behind her ears. "John, do you have a minimum wage in your country?"

"Yes."

"Who sets it?"

"Well," I said and thought momentarily. "The federal government *and* the state government do. The federal government sets a base wage, and the states can set it higher if they choose."

"Who enforces it?"

"Both governments, I think."

"In Amoena Vieta, the same principles are at work. Both governments – the servicement and peoplements – serve as a check, ensuring that the minimums are being supplied to all humans. But the global servicement has the greater responsibility as a check and balance on the local peoplement. That is their major function. They *must* ensure that both sets of minimums are being supplied – the base minimum – the global minimum. Local peoplements may give great minimums depending on their material blessings, and the global servicement would then be responsible for ensuring *that* new minimum is supplied.

"The same system is used for Eternal Rights. Local peoplements can give *more* rights if the majority of the people deem it so. Still, the base minimum of rights must be supplied and the global servicement is responsible for ensuring no local peoplement disservices the people.

"The only other function of global servicement is maintaining peace. It is responsible for guiding against factions cropping up in local peoplements. This function cannot hinder the right to assemble or for human beings to naturally coagulate in groups – which is always permissible. It is only when the small groups that form within a local peoplement take to violence: violence is prohibited by the global servicement. This primarily applies to the group violence of one local peoplement against another: which is strictly forbidden by the global servicement. Violence within the community is primarily the responsibility of the community to remedy. But, if it becomes too much for the local peoplement, global servicement may be petitioned. These sum up the entirety of global servicement's responsibilities: global minimums of services and rights and peace-keeping. The rest of the servicement is left to the local peoplements."

"I think I understand, Sophia," I said as I tried to repeat it all in my mind so that I may remember. "But there is one thing essential to our discourse that you have never defined. What, precisely, are global minimums? I get the gist – the least amount of a good or service that must be supplied to the people. But what *are* they – what goods and what services *exactly*?" and just as I asked the question, the transport slid silently to a stop.

"That is what I am taking you to see so that you may understand, John," she said as she gently embraced my right hand and surged me towards the door of the transport. "Let us go."

CHAPTER 4

ECONOMICS

We got off the transport and were in another lush, green area of Amoena Vieta with a landscape of trees and bushes of every sort. The transport loaded the next group of passengers and quietly whisked away as we began walking down the path that ran in front of the transport station. I remembered my feet feeling hot from the warmth of the gravel and a gentle, cool wind sweeping through that refreshed my body the way a fan sweeps over a room. I could still smell the forest scent, but there was something else mingled with it – something not unpleasant but foreign to the woodsy aroma of the last local peoplement.

As we walked down the path, I saw and heard the voices of Amoenians chatting on the porches and stoops of houses. Children were playing all manner of games and laughing, clearly enjoying the innocence of youth. I also saw little houses that looked like stores with the people coming in and out with bags in their hands.

One of the buildings we passed was taller and wider, looking like a giant in comparison to most of the other smaller buildings on either side. On

the top of it was a large statue of one person picking someone else off the ground – helping them up
with one hand cupped under the person's elbow. I
watched the abundance of activity coming in and
out of the larger building with intense interest.
The transport track ran directly behind the large
building and I saw what looked like miniature
transports coming and going from it all the time.
The miniature transports were small enough to
lift on and off of the track and I figured that that
must be a way for the Amoenians to ensure the
large transport could get by if the small transport
was on the same piece of track at the same time.
The miniature transports were quicker than any
vehicle or moped-esque machine I saw in Amoena
Vieta. Before long, my curiosity got the best of me,
and I asked Sophia,

"What is that building?" I pointed upward
toward the larger building. "The one with the statue
of one person picking another up off the ground...
what's it for?"

"That is a hospital. Every local peoplement has
its hospital. It employs a good portion of the 700
households in every region. In addition to its primary job of treating the ill and wounded, each hospital is responsible for progressing the technology of
the medical profession. Research groups and trailblazers of new treatments are ceaselessly producing

new medications, retesting old ones, and submitting their research findings to the Global Hospital in the heart of Amoena Vieta."

I watched as an older man with dirty-looking clothes limped his way past us, nodded in our direction, and then entered the hospital's front doors.

"Can anyone go there for treatment?" I asked as I watched the old man being welcomed by two individuals at the hospital entrance.

Sophia looked at me with a confused look on her face. She looked at me in such a way as to make me feel like a lunatic for asking such a question. "Of course, everyone can go there for treatment. What kind of caring place for the sick would it be if it didn't treat all the sick who came?"

I felt slightly embarrassed that she might have found my question foolish, so I tried to save face. "A pretty poor caring place. That's not how I meant it, though. What I meant to ask was does everyone receive health care... not just if it's an emergency... but anytime?"

"*Of course*!" She emphatically said with a laugh that made me feel like I'd asked a second stupid question in quick succession. She continued, "How can any society call themselves a just and good one while simultaneously putting a price on such a basic, universal, and essential commodity as good health? By birthright, every Amoenian is given access to the best health care in the world – using the best technology we have at any given time. Health care is a basic minimum – it is essential that all people need to live well – and so it is provided for all. It is part of our Eternal Rights." After speaking, she gestured to a bench in front of the hospital and we both sat down. Another blessed, cool wind caressed our faces as we were seated. I was the first to speak after we sat down.

"But if each local peoplement has their own hospital, aren't some hospitals far more advanced technologically than others? And if they are more advanced, isn't it incorrect to say that everyone is getting the best technology?"

"No," Sophia instantly replied as if she expected the question. "That is one role of the global hospital. In addition to monitoring and serving as a check and balance on the local hospitals, the global hospital continually gathers all the breakthrough methods and treatments. It then disperses them to all other local hospitals in Amoena Vieta. This way, everyone worldwide has access to the most up-to-date technology in health care. It's the global hospital's duty to ensure that all Amoenians, by right, can avoid the curable carnal pains and sufferings caused by aberrations of the mind and body. Access to medical care is undeniably a necessity for a good, comfortable life – a life relatively unhampered by mental or physical ailments. Amoenians decided that all people should, by birthright, have free access to this necessity of life. It is the only compassionate and humane thing to do as a society. The belief demonstrates that the whole of a community cares about each individual in the community rather than solely those who have material excess."

As Sophia spoke, I considered the ramifications of the system. I immediately blurted out the most obvious one I could think of.

"But aren't there all kinds of overcrowding and long waits in your hospitals?"

Sophia shook her head. "No. There are only 700 households in each local peoplement, plus and minus those visiting other local peoplements. Of those 700 households, a good number inevitably seek medicine as a career, and a good number of those are blessed with the skills to perform it. The medical profession is exceptionally attractive to Amoenians because our culture is saturated with the ideology of kindness, humanity, and service toward one another. Those who are dedicated to learning the art of healing one's neighbor and who dedicate one's life to easing the mental and physical torments of the human body are widely honored in Amoena Vieta. This culture and these beliefs systems ensure that there is no overcrowding in our hospitals. In most local peoplements, there are simply too many doctors or aspiring physicians to allow overcrowding or long waits.

"Furthermore, the youth of Amoena Vieta are indebted, by global law, in service to the commonweal for at least two years. These youths are required to do various jobs that engage in the production of minimums for the common good. In every local peoplement, there is an ample population of youth who can also aid the doctors to prevent overcrowding and long waits if they occur, along with our medical students who can be pulled into the hospitals to help as they come close to the end of their education. The youths are indeed not trained doctors or nurses, so they are not required to do those jobs – unless of course those are the jobs they desire to learn. Primarily the youths function as transport drivers and orderlies for the hospital, lightening the load of the doctors and nurses. Thus, there is *always* an adequate supply of labor who maintain and staff hospitals, preventing overcrowding and long waits for services. Each local peoplement has a hospital that must be able to serve all its Amoenians at the same time if that unfortunate situation presents itself."

"I see," I said as I gently ran my finger along the warm, black marble of the bench, "but what you said about the youth – you mean they *have* to work in a certain job?"

"For two-years – yes," Sophia replied as she bent over and picked a daisy that grew alongside the bench. "All youth – sometime during the ages of 18 to 22 – must provide service to the commonweal before they can pursue their own private ventures. It is part of their education in service. Each local peoplement has a department that appoints each youth to a job providing either global or local minimums. The local peoplement determines the place of their work, considering where labor is needed."

"But what about after the two years of service? You said they can pursue their own private ventures?" I asked as I began to grow less disturbed by the mandatory service.

"They are absolutely free from that point forward to do whatever they wish. They may continue their education or employ themselves in any public or private sector job available in their local peoplement. Many choose to remain for several more years in their public service job while completing their education in the private sector they want to pursue. Others stay indefinitely in the public sector job. As I said, it is entirely up to them after the two years of service are finished."

"And no one is exempted from the two years of service?"

"No one. It would not be fair to exempt some. Of course, health considerations and fitness factors are weighed before the local peoplement employs the youth for their two years of service. Those who could not do various jobs would, of course, not be required to do them.

"But the two years of service are mandatory. It serves two primary functions. The mandatory labor is made to ensure that there is ample labor to satiate the global minimums entitled to all Amoenians by the Eternal Rights, and it is also part of every Amoenian's education in service." She paused and gently tucked the daisy on the top of her ear before continuing, "Do you have any other questions before we move on to other facets of the Amoenian economy?"

Of course, I had about a million.

"What are the global minimums?" I boldly asked again because she still hadn't directly answered the question. I felt comfortable enough with her now to be like a stubborn child who wanted the answer to something he didn't know.

"They are the basic necessities that all Amoenians are entitled to by virtue of their humanity. Some are part of the Eternal Rights while others are established by a vote. All basic necessities – those things needed to sustain life – are minimums. Health care, for instance, is undeniably a global minimum. Food and water are as well. These are all covered in the Eternal Rights. Others are not, and they come and go by popular vote. I will discuss them more as we go on. But for now, do you have any other questions about our health care system?"

"Yes," I replied and sat back on the bench to recall it. "You said that the hospitals not only treat the sick but also engage in research for new medications and treatments. What is their incentive, since once they create a new and innovative treatment, the knowledge is dispersed to all?"

Sophia laughed immediately in her soft and sweet way. "Forgive me, John," she said once she gained control of herself, "but I am surprised you would ask such a ridiculous question. I guess it should not be, though, since you are a victim of your environment, and your environment has an economic system very different from ours. Your economic system has clearly shaped your thinking in a way that sees humankind as a means to an end rather than as an end in itself." She paused and took a deep breath before continuing, "There is no one motivation that underlies any human action, and, therefore, there is no single answer to your question. But in Amoena Vieta, our culture has consciously diminished material greed as one of the primary motives for existence. Some Amoenian healthcare professionals do their job for the status that is bestowed upon them for their healing and humanistic labor. Others are trailblazers for new treatments to satisfy their vanity and get a worldwide treatment named after them. Still others – and I say with a fair degree of certainty that most – do it simply for the love of their brothers and sisters in the great human family. And there are even more reasons – more than I can conceive for why they constantly create new treatments. There is no monopoly of motive. But material lust is one motive that is all but eradicated by the design of our system – for the sake of the people. But ask yourself, John, how can a private health care system, whose primary goal is inevitably profit, desire to destroy the very diseases and disorders that fuel their livelihood? This material lust destroys humanity, and Amoenians, therefore, saw the necessity to eliminate it from certain sectors of the economy, more specifically, sectors that directly deal with global minimums. It is greed that, when harvested in the breast of human beings through culture, has proven itself to be the great destroyer of human societies. It pits brother against brother and sister against sister. The accumulation of material wealth, or unitrade, is still possible in our system, and some still make it their life's work in the private sector. But in Amoenian culture and education, it is no longer taught as the goal of life as it was in the days of raw Capitalism." Sophia paused and looked up at the sky, and the sun glinted off her green eyes again. "But I am getting ahead of myself. I will explain all of it to you as we go along. Let's return to our path."

As she finished speaking, she got up and began walking toward the path. A small group of Amoenians walked by as we made our way back to the road. One Amoenian raised his right arm toward us and shouted, "Ciao," as she passed. Sophia and I both yelled, "Ciao" simultaneously in return. And we began walking side by side toward the next destination.

* * *

As we walked, I took deep breaths of Amoenian air, enjoying the fresh, delightful feeling of it filling my lungs. The taste of it... it was like no other air I've ever experienced... it was just so *welcoming*. It tasted something like a freshly made salad or maybe like cool, clear water. No dust, debris, monoxide or general filth that permeates every bit of our air.

I saw children playing their games, and every now and then, Sophia and I would pass a pedestrian as we walked. I grew fond of saying "Hello" to the passing people in every language I could because I knew they could understand it all. I saw lots of little buildings that I hadn't really taken much notice of before – although, when I think about it, they were in every place I passed. Those buildings had the same hospital emblem – one human figure helping another get off the ground.

"What are those buildings, Sophia?" I asked as I pointed toward the one with the hospital's emblem on it.

Sophia turned and looked at me with what seemed to me a slight annoyance. It was as if I had interrupted a beautiful thought. "Those buildings are called community aid houses. They're sometimes private and sometimes public institutions that serve as aids for the remedy of a specific problem amongst the members of the community. People suffering from alcohol and drug addiction, those suffering from mental health afflictions, and those who are grieving are all examples of what those buildings are set up to assist. Of course, each building has one specific function or specialization, and that specialization serves one group. Amoenians believe that all problems are *community* problems since the community is generally thought of as one large family. And so, a problem for one of us is a problem for all of us. That is one of the keystone ideals of our culture and education. The community has a human responsibility to lift any individual who is in dubious battle with an inhuman enemy."

I nodded in comprehension, and we continued our walk. For a short stretch, I noticed a stream running alongside the path, making a soft, soothing sound that mingled with the occasional laughs and joyful screams of nearby children. And as always, where there were Amoenians, there was also the soft hum of Amoenish conversation trickling from their lips and into the air.

As we strolled side by side, Sophia continued,

"The Amoenians have learned that the economic system of a society is an essential ingredient in the lifeblood and culture of that society. Therefore, the economic system must not consist of vague and abstract sets of principles the public knows exists but doesn't know how they work. The economic system *must* be a comprehendible structure whose ideology is rooted in the people's consent. Put simply, the ideology of the economic system can't help but influence the thought of the people, and so the people *must* be the creators of the economic system. Do you understand, John?"

I watched as a cricket skipped across the road in front of us before looking to the side and telling her that I did understand.

"Good. Stop me if you need me to clarify any point.

"The Amoenians have never wavered far from the economic system we implemented from our inception because it seems to provide the best of both worlds from an economic standpoint. The philosophies of Karl Marx and Adam Smith represent the two major poles in economic thought throughout history. This is, of course, omitting the roles of manorialism, feudalism, and mercantilism since none are applicable, feasible, or humane. Marx and Smith were both great economic thinkers in their own right, and each developed concepts that were backlashes to the dominant and oppressive economic forces of their times. However, both philosophies contain tragic flaws that serve to sabotage them. Neither Marx nor Smith were able to account for these flaws. Neither sought the moderation that so often alludes to and evades genius.

"Smith wanted a 'laissez-faire' or *hands-off* economic system where the invisible but inequitable hand of the market determines all of the distribution of goods and services in society. Smith believed that the market of 'quid pro quo,' exchange would, without any human intervention, serve the material needs of the people. In practice, it simply taught individuals to be social Darwinists, vying against each other in a jungle of materialism. Smith's system highlighted and cultivated the vice of greed in humankind, making material wealth the centerpiece of life and inequity the law of the land.

"Marx, on the other hand, wanted a system wherein the proletariat – the working class –could use their collective power to instill an economic system that distributes the goods and services they created more equitably in society. We believe Marx's point of view has the strong potential to limit exploitation and provide equity, but only if there is a fair government that controls these collective resources. Due to the great deal of economic power that often ends up in the wrong hands, and due to the specter of greed that haunts humanity, the power structure in such a system often becomes very corrupted. A corrupt power structure is likely to ignore the principles of equity and may become an oppressive, self-interested entity. Marx's revolution of the proletariat has inadvertently often served as another way for a small part of the people to transform themselves into the new oppressors of the people. Do you understand?"

I thought about all I'd learned in history about how communists were just terrible, so I uneasily nodded my head in agreement.

"Good. The Amoenians could see that neither pole in economic thought – Smith's or Marx's – was perfect. But both philosophies had their strong points.

The Amoenians saw the endless exploitation of human beings run rampant in the Capitalist systems and the horrors of totalitarian governments run rampant in the Marxist systems. That is why we set out to use the necessity of compromise to bring together the two economic philosophies. We sought to design a system in which neither the elevation of material goods over humanity that pervades Capitalist practice, nor the possibility of a small group who seizes power over the many which could happen in Marxist practice, could occur. We decided to call our economic system, Democratism."

"Wait Sophia," I interrupted as my throat gagged with nationalistic pride. "In Amer –," I paused, "In my land, we practice Capitalism. And it's got its problems, sure, but it's still the best system there is…"

"I am not attacking either your economic system or your country, John," she interrupted immediately. "And if I tell you about Democratism and you still prefer Capitalism, then so be it. You do not have to accept anything I say or anything the Amoenians practice. All I ask is that you listen and be fair enough to use your innate powers of reason and give it a chance in thought."

"O-okay," I said, feeling embarrassed after confronting her all of a sudden like that. I didn't really know what had gotten into me. It wasn't done with malicious intent by any means. I regrouped myself and began again, "I'm sorry. But first, tell me what you have against Capitalism. Scores of people where I am from are really defensive about its way of thinking."

"Okay, John. There are three basic flaws that we believe are inherent to the Capitalist system of economics. The first is the cheating of the laborer. The system is virtually designed so that business owners must try in any way possible to cheat their laborers to maximize profit. It is an unavoidable tenet of Capitalism. The second major flaw that we believe is inherent to Capitalism is the massive inequities and polarity of wealth and services that is largely due to the cheating of the laborers. This occurs ceaselessly. The system hinges on social Darwinism. Therefore, it is inevitable that the economically strong and fortunate survive while the economically weak and unfortunate are left behind in squalor. In other words, a small group will inevitably own the majority of the wealth while the majority of people will be left to fight amongst themselves for the crumbs left to them by the small group. The third major flaw is the emphasis on the quid pro quo ideology that spreads throughout all aspects of thought in a Capitalist society. In other words, people can't help but become a means to a material end in Capitalism, and that ideology is one of the diseased roots of inhumanity.

"Let me take each flaw we see and expound on it so that you may understand our viewpoint. The first is the cheating of the laborer that runs rampant in Capitalism. Capitalism rests on a foundation of cheating labor. There are two elements involved in any tangible product – labor and materials. Materials derive their worth from scarcity. That is, the less there is of a material, the higher the price that is put on it. This, we understand, cannot be changed. It is an economic law. The only way to reduce the material's price is to reduce its scarcity – to replicate it. Do you understand?"

"Sure," I said and nodded. We continued walking the gravel path, and I tried to focus intently on her and block out the myriad of objects in the serene nature and the scattered bunches of busy people who surrounded us on either side of the path.

Sophia bit her lower lip and continued, "But materials are only one component of worth. Labor is the other component. Labor is what must be added to the materials in order to sell them. This includes all labor facets that are put into the molding of every material – transportation, advertising, artistry, etc. It is safe to say, then, that every tangible product equals materials plus labor. Those are the two components of worth. Agreed?"

It seemed simple enough. Worth equaled labor plus materials. "Sure, I agree."

"Good." she said as we continued to walk the path. Every once in a while, I would listen to the orchestra of sounds – the katydids, the crickets, bullfrogs – a whole smattering of noises.

"Well, then you understand that if material innovation is lacking – in other words, if Capitalists cannot find cheaper ways to supply a certain material to lower the price of their product, then, by default, they must target labor to lessen production costs of their product. In Capitalism, the producer can only target those two facets of value – materials and labor. Right?"

I thought about it for a short while before responding. "No, not necessarily. A good Capitalist won't target labor no matter what to lower the price. A good Capitalist will abide by wage laws and the government will set minimum wages that Capitalists can pay their workers. That eliminates the problem entirely. Wage laws make it so the Capitalists can only cheat labor to a certain degree."

"Yes, John. That is ideal. And Amoenians have minimum wages for both tiers of our economy for that very reason. But what happens when the producers – the Capitalists – lobby the lawmakers, corrupting them with money. What happens then?"

"The minimum wage won't change... it'll remain stagnant," I answered immediately.

"Exactly."

"But wait, you said you took all the mon–," I paused and corrected myself, "unitrade out of the govern–, I mean, servicement, right? So, then, doesn't that eliminate the problem? Lawmakers can no longer be corrupted by unitrade if it is not a part of your politics. Capitalism is not the problem. Money in the political system is the problem. Just take the money out of the political system, and all is solved. Right?"

"No, sadly, that's not all it will take. So long as producers can access legislators, they can use some bribes to affect policy. That is why in Amoena Vieta, the *people* have the veto power over anything and everything the policymakers enact."

"Okay. So, bribery and the influence of wealth are minimized to the point where it is eliminated in Amoena Vieta. Great, but how does this relate to Capitalism's inherent abuse of labor?"

"I am just showing you one way we have limited the abuse of labor in Capitalism through the role of the servicement. A global minimum of wage – which you said you already have in your government – is just one way. Giving the people the power to veto local legislators' minimum wages, the power to set global minimum wages, and the power to remove corrupt legislators are the other solutions to the abuse of labor we have implemented in Amoena Vieta."

"Yes, I understand all that," I said a little impatiently.

"Good. Now, you have agreed that labor is the only component of a product that the producer has a great deal of control over. Producers must constantly compete to lower their production costs to survive in a capitalist market. Labor, then, is what will routinely be targeted to lower costs. So, you see, built into Capitalism is the natural tendency to abuse labor. Minimum wages that the *people* can update when necessary is one part of the solution to Capitalism's design – but it does not *ensure* the protection of the laborer. And the protection of the laborer is essential to avoid the polarity of wealth that breeds injustice and wreaks havoc upon the structure of a society."

"Wait," I said as I got lost in confusion. "That's not really true," I protested as I felt the drums of nationalism beating in my chest, "many Capitalists pay fair wages to laborers."

"They usually aren't the successful ones," Sophia retorted instantly. "The system's goal is profit – not kindness or humanity, not morality or fairness – only profit. And so, Capitalism's influence on any society will be to turn the business owners into metaphorical animal trainers who try to get their animals to perform the best for the least amount of sleep and food. The business owners – to be successful – will have to learn how to fool their government and to cheat their workers better than the competition. The most successful capitalists will usually be the ones who are best at cheating labor and outsmarting the government.

Labor, in response, has but two avenues – unionization and their servicement, or government. Unionization provides them their best protection, but it, like
the government, is susceptible to corruption through
the temptation of money. Labor's final option, the
government, is usually in the pockets of the business
owners since business owners have the sway of the
almighty dollar over the government. As you can see,
the system is fundamentally set up to abuse labor."

I responded immediately, "But you say that
global minimums, removing the influence of wealth
in politics, allowing people to override the local legislators' minimum, and setting the global minimum
remedies all those problems. So then, why change
the system? It is fixed, isn't it?"

"That aspect of it is, yes. But the built-in abuse of
labor that lies at the very heart of Capitalism is not
all that Amoenians fault. Let me continue..."

I nodded and looked ahead at the path and saw
it was about to wrap around a mountain. As we
passed around to the other side of the mountain, the
soothing sound of the stream surrounded us once
again, and I smiled with a refreshed delight. After a
few moments, Sophia went on,

"The second flaw that we believe pumps at the
heart of Capitalism is a direct result of the first: that
is, the inevitable polarization of wealth that will
occur in any purely Capitalist society."

"Wait a minute," I interrupted, "What's wrong with some polarization of wealth wherein some have a little, and others have a lot? It's diversity – just like you like Sophia! What's wrong with that?"

Sophia laughed lightly and spoke in a soft, didactic voice, "If it were a moderate differential in wealth – some having relatively little while some having a relative lot – it wouldn't be a problem. But Capitalism naturally forms a *wide* gap in wealth, that is, a severe and distinct distribution of wealth. Labor is exploited, and the capitalist reaps the benefit. On a mass scale, this generally results in many laborers living in squalor while the few owners hold the vast majority of wealth gotten through exploitation. Vast numbers of the population will hover near material nothingness while small portions will stand on a mountain of material wealth. And it is common sense that when an uneven distribution of wealth marries any society, injustice will be their child. What kind of commonweal is a society wherein the masses are left to quarrel over the crumbs dropped by the few with all the food? Social injustice reigns supreme when the disparity of wealth becomes vast in a society. And the same occurs when resources are distributed by a corrupt few to the many. Therefore, neither Capitalism nor Communism is advocated by most Amoenians."

"But, Sophia," I objected, "what's so unfair about an uneven distribution? The majority of the people you speak of – can get the things they need, don't they? Capitalism allows everyone to have whatever material item they want so long as they can pay for it."

I saw what I thought was irritation flash across Sophia's eyes as we continued on the path. The soothing sound of the stream served as a backdrop for almost the whole discussion.

Sophia's tone became sterner as she spoke, "It is the condition you put on that last statement: 'if they can pay for it' from which the injustice springs." She took a deep breath and went on, "Let us say... let us *pretend*, for a moment, that the vast portions of people left in need and want had no disabilities and mental illness, no carnal pain and suffering amongst them. Let us pretend for the sake of your argument that these vast portions of human beings were veritable Übermenches or Supermen. Even then, they would have immense difficulty climbing this false notion of an open class system that you allude to without having to overcome *enormous* burdens. These almost insurmountable – and in some cases truly insurmountable – hurdles and burdens are typically removed from the path of those who were born into material comfort – those who reside at the top of the Capitalist pyramid. One needs adequate knowledge to climb this invisible ladder of the Capitalist system. And knowledge, like almost everything in a Capitalist society, has a dollar sign accompanying it that makes it out of reach to large segments of the population. One needs to have all the basic necessities of life – the physiological needs of food, water, and housing *and* the psychological needs of knowledge and love to climb the invisible ladder of the Capitalist market. So, then, it is virtually impossible for a Capitalist society wherein the masses have to fight for these necessities to ask them to climb that ladder unaided. How can society ask one without boots to pull themselves up by their bootstraps? It is not only impossible: it is cruel.

"Amoenians believe every individual is entitled – by Eternal Right – to be given a compassionate hand to help them pick themselves up. We do not eliminate but minimize Adam Smith's invisible hand that allocates resources to the few fortunate and leaves scraps amongst the many unfortunate to fight over. Amoenians do not believe it is natural for all human beings to share equally in all things either. They admire the concept of all things being in common but understand that it is irreconcilable with human nature: greed and the lust for power create constant inequities. But to be given enough: this is that noble ideal on which Amoenians base Democratism. It is an economic system in which every human being, every beating human heart, is ensured the agreed-upon essentials needed not only to sustain life but to cultivate happiness and enrich themselves. Surely you understand the humaneness – the compassion – in this idealistic but feasible principle? To make certain all have *enough* – not the same – but *enough*; to lovingly compensate those who have lost the genetic lottery; to exempt the unfortunate from living a life untouched by Smith's invisible and uncaring hand that would otherwise leave them to wallow in poverty and condemn them to the prison of their own bodies; that is the basis of Democratism. It rests on the keystone that all should be provided with enough by the right of birth. The compassionate wisdom of Democratism was what Amoenians learned from centuries of errors made by the human family. There are differences in material wealth across our land, but the crushing polarity that springs from the heart of Capitalism is forbidden from entering our land."

I listened attentively to her response. It sounded wonderful in theory, but, like all the past utopias, it was just a nice-sounding theory to me. So, I asked,

"How, though, Sophia? I mean, it sounds great and all, but *how* can that be done? How can Amoenians install this humane economic system? How?" I asked again with mounting anticipation.

Sophia bent over and picked a violet flower that was growing alongside the path. She held it gently and spoke, "We will get to that, John. But let us finish our analysis of Capitalism. Let me describe what Amoenians believe is the third fatal flaw of Smith's economic treatise, one that is even greater than the abuse of labor and the polarization of wealth. It is the disease of quid pro quo ideology that spreads like a virus throughout the thought of the culture that Capitalism infects."

I looked across a large, green field that lined the section of the path we were walking. In the wide openness, I watched as a small herd of cattle grazed, and not far from there, a few pigs were eating leaves that lay on the ground next to a nearby tree.

Sophia began the third criticism of Capitalism, and I couldn't help but feel a little embarrassed. I did not know what 'quid pro quo' meant. They never taught us stuff like that in high school, you know?

Sophia did not laugh or anything when I told her I didn't know. She just calmly told me,

"It means *this for that*. It's Latin. Don't be embarrassed that you do not know what it means. Your society should be blushing, not you. Your society is the one that failed to provide you with an education that at *least* covered the basics of one of the most important systems that make up the composition of any society: its economic system. It has been very common throughout history for individuals not to know much about the economic system that influenced both their thought and their actions. And that is tragic. The well-educated citizenry that democracy depends on must know the basic principles of their economic system. It affects everything. Amoenians put a great deal of emphasis on education, which I will show you later. But for now, let it suffice to say there is no one in Amoena Vieta who does not know the basics of all economic systems – but especially their own, Democratism."

I let out a little humble laugh and felt the embarrassment subside upon hearing her tolerance of my ignorance. I asked her to continue explaining quid pro quo, and she went on, speaking slowly and clearly.

"Quid pro quo is the fundamental mechanism that is at work in the Capitalist system. Of course, the practice of quid pro quo predates Adam Smith all the way back to, in all likelihood, the very first human beings. The days of bartering were built on quid pro quo. It is an inevitable mechanism that functions in any economic system because it is so native to humankind: this for that. It says, 'I'll give you this, and you'll give me that.' It's cause and effect. It's very natural. It is the trade that occurred in bartering and mercantilism. It is the keystone of Capitalism."

I thought about it for a few seconds and saw nothing wrong with the practice in any way. "You say it is natural and that it has been a part of so many economic systems in the past. So, then, what is wrong with it? It seems to me it's the way to go."

Sophia shook her head and spoke with conviction, "What's wrong with it is that the 'this for that' ideology does not remain relegated solely to the economic sphere of human relations. The problem is that quid pro quo extends its tentacles deep into the minds of those who practice it. The psychology of it taps into nearly every thought process and behavior of those individuals. Therefore, it spills over into the social relationships of any society that practices it. If it could be kept solely to the realm of material or economic relations between people, quid pro quo may not hurt society as much. It can't help but spill over into the psychological and sociological realms. Therein lays the problem of quid pro quo. It must be kept in check."

I furrowed my brow and looked at her with a sort of disbelieving expression. She continued without addressing the look.

"Let me explain it in more detail, John. I ask only that you listen – not that you believe. Any quid pro quo transaction in the economic sphere is inherently a self-interested transaction. The basis rests on the fact that one party will *only* give something to the other party *if* that other party gives something in return that is perceived to be of equal exchange. In other words, it forms an economic principle in the person's mind that says, 'I must receive something of what I believe to be equal value for whatever I give.' This economic principle seems to fit in with the nature of human beings since we are naturally self-interested to a large extent. That's likely why capitalism is based on this principle, because it preys on this part of the nature of human beings. We can still see this principal in the past and today in every human being. And the system is undoubtedly functional and good in many ways – that is why it has survived this long."

"So, then what's the problem with it?" I asked confusedly.

"The problem is that a functional economic system does not equal a good economic system. Capitalism is most certainly a functional economic system. But it does not encourage or integrate social justice into its ideology. The quid pro quo mechanism that fuels Capitalism opens and cultivates two of humankind's worst and most natural vices: the vices of greed and selfishness. These two vices spawn an 'I'm looking out for me, and I'm going to get what is mine' philosophy. A Capitalist society encourages the accumulation for the sake of accumulation of material goods. It emphasizes self-reliance – which is not a bad thing – but when self-reliance turns into self-interest, people inevitably ignore the well-being of the whole. Smith's system does not only encourage greed and self-interest. The doctrine of laissez faire discourages any intervention by the servicement, or the government, to rectify the wrongs of the greed-driven, quid pro quo market. Thus, the quid pro quo ideology runs rampant, without a check or a balance on it. A society wherein greedy self-interest reigns and the good of the whole is ignored cannot be a commonweal. A society where selfishness and greed are *cultivated* cannot be a commonweal. A society wherein self-interest and greed are patted on the back and considered the virtues of the 'successful' cannot be a commonweal."

"Now hang on Sophia," I said with the national pride rising in me once again, "So what if quid pro quo dominates the economic ideology of a society. That doesn't mean it will infect the social sphere. It's a non sequitur!" I said, using the only other Latin phrase I knew outside of vini vidi vici.

"You make a good point. But the truth is that the principles of any economic system *can't help* but affect all other aspects of society. The cesspool of quid pro quo selfishness will inevitably spill over into the lake of social relations between the members of society. I'm sure you needn't think very hard to see that in the social sphere of your own society, John."

I tried to think of many different instances which would contradict this, but there were so few. In fact, except for selfless charities, there were none who didn't want either material compensation or service for their service or material compensation. "You – you're right, Sophia," I said after a minute or two of thought.

"So, then you understand the third and most deleterious flaw of Capitalism. People will naturally begin to view each other in a quid pro quo manner. They will view their fellow human beings as a means to an end in both the economic and the social spheres. Amoenians believe no single concept is as deleterious to the commonweal as this. The quid pro quo philosophy and the competition that accompanies it make self-interested monsters out of the people. Don't misunderstand, John – competition and self-interest are very wonderful things if kept in moderation. Competition for the necessities of life, in particular, is one of the ways Capitalism can foster an evil kind of self-interest. The more emphasis on *self-interest* and competition for necessities, the less a commonweal can be just – a commonweal. It is the establishment of global minimums that have enabled Amoenians to create an economic system in Democratism that does not consistently birth greed and self-interest in the hearts and minds of the people."

I picked up a small rock on the side of the path and skipped it in front of us. I listened to its clacking noise as I pondered her statement.

"But wait," I said. "How do you know it is Capitalism that causes this 'using' of people in the social realm? You said yourself that quid pro quo was natural to the human race. And you also said that it is probable that from the beginning of humankind, there was a quid pro quo of some sort. So then, how do you know that greed and self-interest are not just the normal state of human beings – whether there is a quid pro quo in their culture or not? Can't human beings be the problem and not quid pro quo or Capitalism? I don't think people would exactly be holding hands and singing if Capitalism were not their economic system. I don't think people are naturally *that* good."

Sophia laughed in a louder way than I had ever heard her laugh the entire time I was with her. "You pose a very good question, John. It's the question of the chicken or the egg, really. Are people naturally self-interested and greedy – so much so that Capitalism fits their innate composition like a glove? Or is it the other way around – does the quid pro quo mentality that children are indoctrinated with become the status quo of thought and spread to all areas of action? I will tell you the truth," she said as she turned and paused and looked me right in the eye, "Amoenians cannot definitively answer that question because it is an unanswerable one. The reasoning of Amoenians on the issue has always has been as follows...

"No one can say with certainty what the natural instincts of human beings are in large part because not all human beings share any one instinct other than the instinct to satiate certain needs: many of which Democratism does satiate. But through the powers of observation and logic, Amoenians *can* definitely say that the quid pro quo mentality, carried over into the social realm, has served as a catalyst for people to view people not as human beings but merely as means to a self-interested end."

I stood confusedly, and she clarified immediately.

"What I'm telling you is that it does not matter whether human beings are, on the whole, innately selfish. If they are, teaching Capitalist ideology to the people of the society is something like pouring gas into a flame. The self-interested keystone that reigns in capitalist thought will turn a great deal of people into greedy, selfish monsters if that is the case. If people are not innately self-interested and greedy, Capitalism's ideology will drive most of them toward selfishness and greed. Either way, the capitalist ideology is not wise to encourage in the human heart. It breeds selfishness and greed in the thought of the economic realm. The economic realm can't help but affect the thought of the psychological and sociological realms. Once quid pro quo reigns in the psychological realm, people begin to view each other as objects to be manipulated toward a self-interested end rather than as people. Quid pro quo in the social realm is the stepping stone to horrendous inhumanity and the slow but sure devolution of any society it dominates. That's why Amoenians aim to nip this ideology in the bud while cultivating selflessness and humanity. We can only do so through the blessed conduits of knowledge and education. Don't misunderstand, John, some degree of quid pro quo is unavoidable in any economic system. We did not intend or think it possible to eliminate it altogether. This-for-that is too simple and based on the laws of cause and effect. Quite simply, it is too readily available to logic and reason to weed it out of the human psyche. Amoenians only hope to limit and contain self-interest and its relative greed so that it is a mere segment of the economic and social thought of the people instead of it serving as a keystone. Capitalism cultivates and highlights these destructive human vices while Democratism minimizes and deemphasizes them. Amoenians also encourage all kinds of economic thought and hoped to produce a more perfect and just economic system." Before I could say anything, she added, "So you see, Amoenians generally do not take the position that people are basically good or bad in the designing of their systems. There is too much variation on that question to get a definitive answer across the population. But it is pretty much agreed upon that while people have in them the capacity for greed and self-interest, they also have in them the capacity for generosity and selfless love. Capitalism cultivates the former two vices and suppresses the latter two values. And this is antithetical to the idea of a commonweal. We have designed a different system that better serves the idea of a commonweal."

"And it is called Democratism," I said a little impatiently. "That's the system. I got that. What I don't get is how it works."

Sophia reached up and tugged on a branch hanging from a tree. She inspected the green leaf momentarily before letting it go, springing branches back into their previous position.

"And I will show you. We are almost there."

* * *

Before long, we came to a large, rectangular building further back and isolated from the rest of the local peoplement. Large deciduous trees were in front of the building on either side, parallel to each other. I could see many thin, red lasers between the trees, across the path, and on the sides of the building as well. Sophia told me to stay where I was and she walked up to an intercom that stuck out of the ground just before the first laser. She uttered a few words in a language I could not understand, and before I knew it, all the lasers disappeared.

We walked quickly to the front of the rectangular building, and as we got closer, I could see two other little buildings on either side. Each smaller building was also rectangular and white and neither stood very high off the ground. On the top of the main building, I could see a marble statue similar to the ones in all the community centers in the local and global capitals. The marble sculpture was a fountain spewing liquid. Underneath the fountain of liquid was a group of people sculpted in marble underneath, catching drops of the liquid. Sophia waved her hand in front of the doors of the building and they slid open immediately. We went in.

The first thing that struck me was the smell. It smelled like bleach or chlorine, like a swimming pool. Four huge, rectangular pools of water took up the vast majority of the room. At the bottom of each pool, I saw two big, round, circular tubes. From one tube, I could see a water current being sent into the pool and the other, I assumed, was sucking water down and out. Around each side, there were people – workers, wearing blue overalls, all busy doing something to the water. Two were on each shorter end of the rectangular pools and four lined each longer end. Every one of the workers on the rim of the pools held paddles – wooden paddles – and they were continuously stirring the water in a clockwise circle. Around each pool, there were also two additional workers circling the pool constantly and occasionally dropping something into the water. Each pool had one person who was dropping little white cubes that looked sort of like cubes of salt. And the other person was occasionally dropping some kind of white powder into the water. Two *more* workers were dressed in blue overalls, each holding a vial and continually filling it with water from each pool.

After I surveyed the whole scene, Sophia finally began to speak,

"Welcome to one of the many water purification plants in Amoena Vieta, John. Every local peoplement requires one to cleanse the drinking water, bathroom water, and any other type of running water needed for a home."

I took another look around the rectangular room and saw other workers. Some were old, but most were younger. There was, for instance, one man who had another man watching over him – as if he were the supervisor and the other man were the employee. But most of the workers looked like young adults. They looked like young men and women who were at their first job. It was then I realized that the women and men probably *were* at their first job. It was probably part of the two years of commonweal service that all Amoenians must do. I pointed to a tall young man with curly dark hair and asked, "Are these women and men part of the two-year public service group... the one you told me about before?"

She nodded immediately. "That's right."

I glanced at the many workers in the room. Some were talking with each other in a low hum, others were working diligently, and still others were just standing there idly and looking at the water. After some time, the workers all switched jobs – those talking became the ones just standing there looking at the water, the ones working were talking, and the ones standing were then working diligently. I heard a loud, high-pitched whistle blow each time the change occurred.

I took a deep inhale of the chlorine smelling air before I continued, "Is water a public item, free to all? Is water one of the global minimums you were talking about?"

"Yes," she said. "It is undeniable that water is a necessity for all. Therefore, it is an Eternal Right, and an adequate amount is freely distributed to all."

"You say an 'adequate' amount is supplied to each person as a global minimum. How much, though, is adequate?"

"That is what is voted on each year. The popular vote in the global elections determines the global minimum of water. The amount that can be supplied is determined by several independent study groups that estimate the amount of production capabilities for every local peoplement and take human needs into consideration – such as what the average human need is for water – for drinking, bathing, bathroom uses, etc.

"The independent study groups that determine the production capacity of water are similar to the other independent study groups of scientists and specialists who determine the production capacity of other global minimums such as food and clothing. They measure such things as current technologies, the number of the items on the earth, work capacity, etc., to determine voters' options when voting for global minimums. This is the basis for all publicly made goods – and all publicly made goods are those that are free to the population to a certain extent – determined by global and local minimums. And all goods that are free to the public are those goods that are necessary to live, in addition to any other universal items that the popular vote has deemed should be publicly supplied. Of course, public demand must never increase beyond the supply. That is what the many independent groups determine when they are given the options the populace has for global minimums each year. Due to the fluctuating labor supply caused by differences in the young 18–22 year-old population and the turnover in career public workers, the global minimums for necessities must constantly be adjusted. This is the basis of the first tier of our two-tiered economic system. It is the tier that is influenced by Marx and is considered the public tier. It absolutely ensures, barring an act of nature, that every citizen has enough of everything needed to sustain and cultivate life. It also ensures that every citizen has a job. If a citizen is unable to find work in the private sphere, then that citizen is guaranteed work in the public sphere. Outside of the two mandatory years that the youth must work in the public sphere, *there is no obligation for any Amoenian to ever work in the public sphere of our economy again,*" she said in an obvious attempt to emphasize the economic freedom Amoenians have after those two years.

I watched a large man come out of the room in the back and begin talking loudly to one of the boys who was dropping the white cubes into the pool. He took the cube and talked to the boy as he put it into the water. I quickly realized he was demonstrating how often the boy *should* put the cubes into the water for purification.

'But wait," I said as I thought about the system Sophia described, "How can that be? If there are only so many public products – global minimums – then there are only so many public jobs available. And with all the young people having to put in two years of work at public jobs, I don't really see how there could be all that many jobs to go around."

"Well thought out John," Sophia said, and I stood there beaming with a feeling of intellectual pride. "But the Amoenians had anticipated that prospective problem and adjusted the economic structure to deal with it...

"If, at any time, due to cultural or natural changes, there is a surplus of Amoenians working in the public sphere, the Amoenian people will vote on a global decree into law that states the mandatory public service that the youth must do. This reduction of many, and sometimes all, of the public jobs that the youth normally fill has always created enough work for the full employment of all Amoenians who *can* work. And the public sphere always functions at a capacity that produces enough global minimums for all Amoenians. That is the golden rule of Democratism – *that everyone always has enough*. After this baseline is achieved, one can live whatever economic life they want. They can, if they choose, pursue as much wealth as he or she desires in the private tier of Amoenian economics. That is the section of the

Democratist economy directly influenced by Adam Smith."

I thought about it but doubt still clouded my mind. "There are a lot of public jobs here, Sophia. And there are a lot of global minimums that are produced, from what I'm hearing. Global minimums cost a lot to produce because the labor and materials all must be purchased. So, then, who is paying for it all? Who pays the salaries for all these public jobs that create goods for everyone?" I said as I watched another young man drag a net through one of the pools of water, catching debris.

Sophia laughed, "The commonwealth pays for it, of course. These jobs are necessary for the good of all, and so these jobs are paid for by all. Using a progressive scale, a certain amount of unitrade is chipped in by every Amoenian to pay the workers who provide the global minimums."

"But how is that fair?" I asked, hearing the same objection my grandparents always had coming out of my throat. "Why should some have to pay more than others for the global minimums?"

"Because Amoenians generally agree on one of the teachings of whom many consider the greatest teacher, Christ. He spoke of much being expected of those who have been given a great deal. We apply this philosophy to the commonweal. Some members of society have been given much – whether by winning the genetic lottery, by good circumstance, or by some combination of the two. And so, since they have been given more than their brethren in society, they are expected to chip in more to society for the well-being of those who haven't been given as much. It is simple humanitarianism, really. In fact, it is the *only* humane thing to do. Amoenians generally believe that the strong have an obligation to pick up the weak for the benefit of all."

"That makes sense," I nodded as I watched four more Amoenians sprinkle a white powder – different from the cubes – in the many pools of water as soon as the whistle blew for the next rotation. "You just used a religious figure to justify an Amoenian point. But I thought Amoenians didn't mix servicement with religion? I thought everyone was free to believe what they wanted?"

Sophia replied as if she expected my question. "They can. There is no real religious implication there. I only used a religious figure you knew well to illustrate the point. It is the veracity of the philosophy that is the issue. And the existence of that veracity is really a moral question, not a religious one. Morals and servicement can never be separated. Religion and servicement can be separated for the good of all – but morality and servicement, or government, can *never* be separated, John."

As I listened, I watched two stout women standing near one of the vats and talking to each other. Both women – one younger and one older – held glasses full of water. The slightly taller and more vibrant younger woman was sipping from one of the two glasses she held. The other, older woman also drank from her glass but at a much quicker pace. The older woman drank the entire two glasses of water that she held in the time it took the younger woman to sip away half of one glass. The women and the water drinking spurred a question in my mind as I watched. I asked Sophia, "But what about Amoenians who consume more than other Amoenians naturally? What about Amoenian families who have more members than other Amoenian families… how does your system, Democratism, account for that? You can't honestly suggest that they all – big families and little – get the same global minimums as if they all had the same biology, physiology and so on. That would not only be unnatural – but I'd say it was just plain cruel to give a 5'10, 150-pound person the same global minimum to use as a 6'2, 250-pound person!" I said and smiled to diminish the sarcastic tone I heard in my voice. "What I mean is that's the major reason I can see for global minimums not working – because not everyone should get the same basic amount of anything – because they are all so different and need different amounts of each thing.

That is one of the main reasons having all things in common doesn't seem to ever work. It's not practical or even right for everyone to have the same."

Sophia looked at me with her eyebrows raised and a kind look in her eyes before she started to speak, "You're right. And Amoenians would not base even an aspect of Democratism on the ideal that everyone have the same. As I've explained, we borrow from Marx, but we borrow from Smith too – the public sphere is only a *portion* of our two-tiered economy," she said and then paused and tilted her head back before continuing, "But now let me address your other questions. You say that some consume more than others of the global minimums, and you are undeniably correct. The diversity of actions and thoughts, beliefs and compositions of the human being seems almost limitless: and that is not something that the servicement should ever try to change. Amoenians always have and will continue to cultivate the diversity in humankind and not infringe upon it. It is guaranteed in the Eternal Right: To thine own self be true – this is not just an attitude and belief, but also a psychological need.

"That's why the global minimums are just that– minimums used to sustain a healthy life. For some, the minimums are too much, while for others, they are too little. For those who find the amount of a minimum not to satiate their needs, they are free to purchase more on the free market tier of our economy. They are also free to petition those individuals in the community who have received more than they can use. But the minimums are composed in such a way that everyone is given at least enough to live, and for most people, the minimum is a very comfortable amount. So yes, people need different amounts of each global minimum, yet they receive the same amount that everyone else is receiving. However, Amoenians are completely free to accumulate more of any global minimum on the free market tier of our economy if it is desired. They automatically receive *but are not limited to* the global minimum."

Sophia cleared her throat and swallowed before continuing,

"Your second criticism pertained to global minimums and the diversity of family sizes. That is taken into account when Amoenians vote for global minimums. *Every person* is guaranteed a base amount of every global minimum: not every family. Thus, there is no scarcity for any Amoenian family of any global minimum: each *individual* receives a livable amount of each global minimum. It is not as if we give a family of four the same as a family of six – the family of six is given enough global minimums to satiate two more individuals. This ensures that every person always has enough and, consequently, that Eternal Rights are guaranteed."

I nodded, and Sophia instantly started toward the door of the water purification plant. "Come on, John, let's go," she said, and I followed hurriedly. I turned back and took one last look at the workers bent over and studying the pools of water in the plant. And it was at that moment that I was stunned by the epiphany that *there were no machines*, with the exception of the pump that brought the water in and out of the pool. As I followed Sophia out the door, I asked, "Sophia... I just realized... there are no machines other than the pump! Can't Amoenians build machines to do all or at least most of the water purification? Why employ all these people when machines could do it? There are lots of workers here and most of this work could be done by machines like it is where I come from."

Sophia stopped just after we got outside of the plant's front door. She turned around in such a way a mother does when she is upset with her son for saying a bad word. Her eyes looked at me as if I were an idiot. But then her face softened, and I caught a glint of the bright green of her eyes when the sun blessed them as she spoke. "The question you have asked is one that sprouts from the surly bonds of the Capitalistic ideology that preaches profit even at the cost of human welfare, John. *Why* would we employ machines instead of people? Do machines need a wage? Do they need to eat and drink and be nourished? Do machines think and have a need to sustain their own lives?"

I shook my head. "Well of course not but –"

"Then why would we replace our laborers with machines – with entities needing no unitrade? What would our priorities be if we let a machine do the labor that could earn a human being the material profit that could enrich her or his life?"

"So that the servicement could increase production *and* save the people money in taxes," I replied immediately and confidently. "It's the same concept behind why businesspeople incessantly replace their more expensive labor with either cheaper labor or mechanical labor where I'm from: it's cheaper."

"Yes, but you see, you are from a place where Capitalism reigns like an evil specter over people's ideology, a place where profit is defined as *material* gain rather than *humanitarian* gain. In Amoena Vieta, the primary profit our system is concerned with is the profit of the *commonweal*. Great profit is measured by the satisfaction and goodness of knowing that every beating heart has the basics of life, knowing that it is assured that there is a job for every hand, knowing that we will never stop trying to alleviate the problems life places on all our brothers and sisters. *That* is generally what Amoenians consider profit John, not unitrade."

I nodded, and my eyes were instinctually attracted to the movement of a grasshopper as it skipped across the minor path that led us back to the major path. The laser that guarded the front of the water purification plant vanished upon our stepping outside, and once we reached the path, Sophia began speaking again,

"Now, as I said, this," she motioned toward the purification plant, "is an example of one of the public tiers of our economy. There is only a very minimal amount of unitrade that can be earned for this work."

"Then how are these workers motivated?" I asked immediately.

"Ideally, they are motivated by the goodness of providing a necessity for all. But this is not the case for many workers. Despite the Amoenian education and culture that puts a great deal of emphasis on altruism, the vice of selfishness still resides within a great many – if not all – people. That is unavoidable even if it is discouraged by society and it will likely always remain in the human psyche – which is, in some ways, desirable because it is human. However, that particular vice is amongst the most destructive to the commonweal of a society. That's why the general goal of Amoenians as a group is not to eliminate selfishness – to minimize it, yes – but not to eliminate it. We want to do nothing that destroys self-expression," she said before pausing as if trying to remember what she was saying. "But to answer your question, the public workers are motivated primarily by the surplus of minimums – of public goods – that they are allowed to have as servicement workers. They are given more water and food as a reward and privilege for their work for the servicement. Many public servicement workers trade the excess they are allowed to have by virtue of their position to individuals in the private sector for unitrade. In other words, the benefits they get from this job can be made into extra unitrade very easily. For instance, some public workers open small shops in the private tier and sell the excesses they are given. *This* is their added motivation for those who need more reason to work in a public job producing global minimums for the good of all. But it should be noted that a great many of these workers need no more payment than the minimums they receive and the goodness they feel for the noble job they are doing for their brothers and sisters in society."

"I see," I said as we walked the road. "How many of the 700 households in each local peoplement work in public jobs?"

Sophia paused with a furrowed brow for a few moments before speaking. "It is never the same for each local peoplement. It all depends on what the people want it to be – some peoplements have a much larger amount of local minimums than others – and the creation of local minimums requires public jobs. The numbers of individuals who work for the public sector in each peoplement is also dependent on how many young adults are available to do their two years of public service and upon how many prisoners the peoplement has to do work."

"You mean *criminals* work there – work purifying the water and making food and any other minimums the people are assured? *Criminals*?" I said, almost gagging in protest.

Sophia stopped her walk immediately. She turned and looked at me as if I were a lunatic. "*Of course* we have them work for the common good. How do you think it should be structured? Would you have them sitting idly in a cell, learning from others how to be a better criminal?"

"Well... no. But it seems they shouldn't be in public jobs – handling our necessities like food and water."

"Each prisoner who does labor for the commonweal is supervised individually by an Amoenian official from one of the oversight groups. You did not comment on it, but there was a man who was overseeing a prisoner in the water treatment plant you just came from. The system is remarkably safe because of the close supervision. You also saw them alongside the roads we've walked, cleaning and picking up garbage, improving the overall quality of the roads and, therefore, the overall quality of the commonwealth. The public asserts that prisoners are *required* to do work to help them cultivate a sense of community and responsibility. That principle – the amelioration of the prisoner – is what Amoenians have generally decided should be the goal of any institution that calls itself *corrections*. Corrections should do that – correct – rehabilitate – teach. In the societies of the past, we have found corrections were institutions of punishment without education for the betterment of the individual. In these institutions, prisoners learned only to become better criminals.

"Of course, the prisoners do not receive the benefits the other workers receive. They are not paid the same, and they do not receive the benefit of surplus that the other workers receive. They are also deprived of freedom and the occupational choice that all other Amoenian public employees have. The program is simply a way of making something good out of something bad – educating while detaining these individuals for the commonweal. It is instilled the entire time they are in prison, and once they are finished, they are granted back any rights taken away from them while imprisoned. All prisoners do retain their Eternal Rights – with the exception of those Eternal Rights that pertain to carnal, or bodily,

– freedom, since carnal freedom is what has to be infringed upon to protect the whole of society. No humane society treats its criminals as if they have lost their humanity. Amoenians generally view those who have hurt others or society as people who have lost their way on the road of personal expression. They remain part of our family nonetheless and are given respect and treated humanely. An evil done by a criminal does not merit evil done by the common-weal. There is no logic in that because evil cannot drive out evil. The public service criminals are made to do has been a wonderfully effective tool in their rehabilitation, and it is constructive for both the criminal and the society."

When she finished talking, I nodded my head. The explanation seemed both logical and just. After a moment, she gestured for me to come near her and said, "Come on, John, I want you to see where the other fifty percent of Amoenians produce goods – in the private tier of Democratism's two-tiered economy. Come, see how the other citizens in a peo-plement work for their livelihood."

* * *

We came to a small white and grey building on the side of the path. On it was a little worn-out wooden sign.

I don't know what language it was or what it meant. My first guess was that it meant "restaurant" or "food" or something like that because everybody inside seemed to be eating. And the walls on each side of us were decorated with drawings... murals of human figures eating, drinking, laughing and talking. And the entire place was filled with a smell – it was of brown rice and vegetables or something like that. There were people sitting and eating in almost every seat, and I heard words here and there of English mixed with every other language I'd heard, some of which I couldn't identify.

A younger man came to our table as I continued to survey the scene like a kid in Santa's workshop. The man was thin, muscular, and wore a black T-shirt with a little pocket. Sophia said a few words to him, and the man immediately nodded and walked to the counter. I watched as the young man leaned over the counter and said something to a portly man with jet-black hair encircling a large bald spot on the top of his head. The portly man nodded and handed the boy two cups, and the next thing I knew, I was drinking the cold water the waiter had brought over.

"This is a deli, John," Sophia finally said to me. "I've taken you here to show you the other tier of our economy – the private tier."

"Right – you said that. This is where the rest of the Amoenians work, then?"

Sophia laughed a soft, pleasant laugh. "Well, not *here,* of course, but places like this, yes. Amoenians are encouraged to create all manner of products in the private tier of our economy for consumption – with one caveat. The products the private tier makes cannot be made *specifically* for the use of hurting, maiming, or killing other human beings."

"So, you mean they can't make weapons?"

"That's right. No knives or guns, or weaponry of any kind is permitted by Amoenians in any people-ment. It is a global law. Amoenians have generally come to the realization that weapons merely serve as temptations for people to destroy the commonweal and each other upon the whims and fluctuations of their emotions."

I stopped drinking the cold water right in the middle of her sentence. "You mean *no one* is allowed to have weapons? Even the police and the govern –" I corrected myself, "servicement aren't allowed to have weapons?"

"I mean that, *especially* anyone who serves the servicement is not allowed to have weapons," she said definitively.

"But that should be a peoplement choice, shouldn't it?" I protested.

"No. What if one peoplement chooses to disallow all residents from having weapons while another allows weapons? Can you see a possible conflict, John?"

"Of course... one peoplement would be able to overtake the other... but still, isn't it a personal choice for the residents of each peoplement? I mean, won't education be the remedy for all problems concerning weapons?"

"No," Sophia replied with conviction. "That is one issue that could not be left solely to the local peoplements. It is too dangerous to the viability of the commonweal. You see, the history of humanity has taught us that humanity's will toward destruction – their *Thanatos* or death instinct – can be *lessened* by education – but not eradicated. Education can lessen or alter but not override innate drives. It can temper those drives in many individuals.

"Our education does temper violence. But it cannot eliminate it. Therefore, we lessen the magnitude of violence between individuals by disabling individuals from using the most destructive human forces. In other words, we have collectively removed the most powerful vehicles of human destruction from our midst."

I saw just a few of the infinite injustices committed by my own government upon the governed play in my mind. "But if the people are not allowed to have weapons by global servicement law, aren't you ultimately just enabling the possibility of the government or servicement or whatever you want to call it to suppress the people?"

Sophia took another sip of water before replying, "Of course not! Amoenians understand that the worst of all possible governments is a police state. All manner of precaution is taken against the manufacture of weapons across Amoena Vieta by the appointment of a myriad of watchdog committees. Any kind of device used to quell individuals by violent means is illegal for Amoenians to privately own – and this law applies *especially* to members of the servicement. Amoenians have learned that violence only leads to violence and that it is amongst the most destructive forces to the commonweal. The only substances that can be used by the people or their servicement are nonviolent gases to quell large groups temporarily. As always, the people control the administration of any nonviolent substance that is allotted to the servicement."

I sipped from my glass and let the ice-cold water trickle down my throat. "So, then, you keep order in society with sleeping gases and other non-injuring substances? That's *it*?" I asked with a sense of shock.

"Not exactly. We will get to the Amoenian legal system. Let it suffice to say that Amoenians have infinitely reduced the inhumanity human beings perpetrate on one another by collectively eradicating the vehicles they can use to satisfy their occasional surges of anger with one another. It is as if everyone has pillows to fight with in lieu of guns and knives. It provides for a much more humane society.

"But I am afraid we have departed too far from the muse of our discourse – Democratism. Let me continue as I was before we wandered from the path of our economic discussion."

I nodded in agreement.

"Amoenians are free to pursue whatever means of economic production are desired with the exception of that rule – their product must not be designed or easily used to injure human beings. And while the private market is where many Amoenians conduct their employment, many work in a combination of public and private venues. A woman may produce art to sell, for instance, in addition to her daily employment at the food sanitation plant. A great deal of Amoenians have a mix of jobs – one foot in the public sector, adding to the good of the commonweal, while the other foot is in the private sector, cultivating their talents for material gain."

I took another sip of water and watched as a tall, lanky man at the next table spoke to a waitress. "What kinds of jobs are there in the private sector – besides," I motioned to the waitress, "food service?"

"Democratism fosters almost every job that exists in a Capitalist economy. Any commodity that is not a *need* is produced in the private sector. Jobs range from management, business and financial occupations, computer and mathematical jobs, architecture and engineering, social sciences, judicial occupations, education, design, entertainment, sports, media, maintenance, personal care, sales, forestry, construction, repair, and other production occupations; all compose part of every peoplement's workforce under the Democratist system." She listed the occupations by rote without so much as taking a breath. Her knowledge of the structure of the economic system of Amoena Vieta seemed to exemplify the emphasis Amoenians put on the economic education of its citizens.

"There is not that much of a difference, then, in the private sector of Democratism and Capitalism?"

She laughed with an innocence native to most children. "There is all the difference in the world between the Democratist and the Capitalist systems in the private sector. Democratism *consciously* destroys or minimizes the three intrinsic flaws of Capitalism that I described earlier while still maintaining a largely free market system in the private tier."

"How, exactly, can it remedy the three flaws you named before – the abuse of labor, the inequity of pay, and the quid pro quo mentality?" I asked before sipping again from my water. After every few sips that Sophia and I took, the thin young man in a black shirt came over with a pitcher to refill our glasses without interfering with our conversation. I made sure to nod gratefully each time.

"We apply the same ideals that we use for our commonweal to the economic system that governs our commonweal. For instance, we use reason and a finely tuned system of checks and balances to make labor virtually unexploitable. More precisely, we make labor exploitable only if there is a complicit agreement of the laborer being exploited. The worker actually has to virtually *accept* and promote her or his own exploitation in order to be exploited. That is how difficult exploitation becomes in the Democratist system."

"How does it work?" I asked curtly.

"In Amoena Vieta, unions are mandatory for all sectors – private and public. The ability for the workers to band together to fight economic injustice is an economic *right* and obligation – not a privilege. There is no union leader who can be cajoled and manipulated by material temptations to betray the union. Instead, the union itself negotiates with the management via the computer. A democratic vote is taken on any major issue. The union is in charge of setting minimums that must be agreed to and satiated by the owners or the manager in both private and public sectors. If agreements cannot be reached between the two sides, an elected mediator who serves the peoplement is brought in."

I looked at her in confusion.

"I will describe mediators much further when we discuss the legal system. Suffice to say that they are elected officials who arbitrate problems throughout the peoplement."

I nodded and she continued,

"The mediator must take an intensive look at the aggregate assets of the business when deciding whether the union's demands are fair. Both the management and the laborers must agree by majority vote on the terms the mediator makes. The mandatory unionization and mediation systems are the first wave of checks to prevent the exploitation of the laborer. They are successful at resolving about 90% of disputes."

"Seems reasonable," I said. "It's something like my uncle's road-workers' union."

"Right. But not *all* disputes can be resolved this way. Compromising can serve as a blessed remedy to most human conflicts – but it is not always achievable. And so, Amoenians have an elected labor commission of citizens in every peoplement. The group is composed entirely of residents within the peoplement – as is every other watchdog commission. This group is charged with the responsibility to decide any worker/management disputes that reach it – those ten percent of cases that no compromise can remedy."

"Aren't they the same as the mediator, then? I mean, that group decides what the terms may be – just like a mediator..."

"Yes, but there is a key difference between mediators and labor commissions. Mediators attempt to facilitate compromise between the two groups and can only provide *suggestions* for compromise between both sides. Mediators have no ability to enforce. Labor commissions, on the other hand, have legal authority. The commonweal grants them the final say– they can immediately end a dispute between labor and management. Labor commissions take the mediator's suggestions into account and usually rule similarly. For those ten percent of cases where labor or management cannot agree on terms, labor commissions are where the path ends. They have the final say.

"It is increasingly rare for disputes to reach the labor commission in the private sector. Most cases are agreed upon and settled in the negotiation and mediation phases of labor disputes in the private sector. In the public sector, however, many more cases reach the third and final arbitration phase. That is because the time limits set on the resolutions and compromises are much more limited in the public sector since the public sector is responsible for creating vital products for the public good. The commonweal cannot afford stubborn and unreasonable disputes between management and labor. Thus, the process is expedited."

"I see. But why do so few of the private labor disputes go to the labor commission?"

"Because the labor commission is like a jury. They have the power to enforce their decisions via the peoplement. In other words, what they rule goes. It is like a lottery for both management and labor to allow the arbitration to reach the labor commission. Therefore, it is generally avoided by both sides. Furthermore, private firms have no mandatory time limit to reach a compromise because they are not making a necessary product for the commonweal. They are able to take their time if they so choose and reach a conclusion that all can accept."

My mind automatically leaped back to the never-ending story of the abuse of labor. My family even once watched as a union leader sold out the union for his private enrichment. The Amoenians completely omitted that by eradicating the union leader – by making the democratic vote the union leader. But the mediators and the labor commissions – they were bribable insofar as I could detect. So, I asked, "Can't management use the almighty dollar to just petition the labor commission or the mediator? Those groups are just as corruptible as any, right?"

"No, John," Sophia said before slowly brushing a loose strand of her dark hair behind her ear. "Great precautions are taken to avoid corruption in our system. Mediators are elected but cannot be petitioned directly by any resident throughout their term. The labor commissions are accessible to the public, though. If there is any conflict of interest – if management is close friends with a member of the labor commission, that member of the labor commission is automatically removed from the case. Conscious and obvious favoritism cannot play a role in our commonweal." As she finished, she took another drink from her glass and loudly gulped it down.

"But still," I protested, stunned at this different way of protecting labor, "even with all these precautions, there must be *some* injustice that labor – that the masses – endure under the Democratist system." By the time I finished that single statement, Sophia's glass was already being refilled by the wonderfully attentive waiter.

"In the course of human events, there will always be injustices that appear in any system. It is true that human beings have a remarkable ability to conceptualize and solve their own problems by designing functional systems that govern their society. But it is also true that the same brilliance – the same necessity – that empowers humanity to produce better systems in society, can also work to find loopholes in those systems. The use of the mental gifts of some individuals to bend any system's rules for their own selfish gain is natural and inevitable. The intelligence bestowed upon humanity is truly a double-edged sword. But Democratism is designed to protect labor while preserving some degree of economic individualism. It does so better than any economic system in the past. Democratism neither places the plight of the working masses in the hands of a small group of individuals nor does it throw the plight of labor into the unfair torrents of a free market ruled by business owners seething with their own self-interest.

"Even on a personal level, every laborer is protected. Every laborer can, at any time, covertly petition the labor commission to review their case – without a need to consult the union as a whole. This step in the collective bargaining process is often taken before the laborer consults the union. The labor commission is obligated by law to review it. The worker can also petition the union if desired. And if all else fails, the worker can approach her or his representative in the local peoplement and/or global servicement. In other words, there are many avenues to destroy the injustices wrought upon labor."

As Sophia concluded, I heard a short, freckled, dark-haired woman speak angrily in Amoenian. My eyes remained fixed while she used both hands to fiercely gesture as she conveyed her point to the man across from her.

Sophia continued without waiting for a response, "Another provision for the regular person is the presence of global minimums. These address the second major flaw of your capitalist system – the wildly uneven distribution of wealth."

"But these global minimums are not necessary, Sophia. Where I'm from, we don't really have them much at all, and the system works wonderfully."

Sophia shook her head in way that reminded me of maternal disapproval. "You say things are 'fine,' John, but I fear that is only because you are not amongst the population for which things are not fine. How easy it is to push out of consciousness those aspects of our society that we do not wish to admit exist!

"Amoenians institute global minimums because we believe it is the right of each person to have enough in the material realm once they are thrown into this world. It is a humanistic tenet, a tenet borne out of concern for others. Humanism is the idealistic ground on which our economic system is based. And remember, John," she said, her eyes filled with a stern, honest look, "human beings must always strive for ideals. It is true that ideals are seldom attainable, but they keep the metaphorical bar of achievement raised highly. Our dreams cannot waver if we are to attain them. Pragmatism is good and needed. But idealism planted in the garden of goodness and hope is what drives forth true progress in the human race. It is what enables us to keep reaching high and making things better. Understand?"

I nodded.

"However, idealism and humanity are not the sole basis for global minimums for all necessities. There are other grounds for global minimums, pragmatic grounds. Global minimums also help regulate our economy by limiting the polarization of wealth. By limiting the polarization of wealth, the global minimum ensures that the masses will be contented and not resort to destroying the system altogether. If people always have enough, which they are assured under our system, then they will not revolt and destroy the system. In other words, our system is designed with compassion so it will not necessitate its own destruction caused by the alienation of the masses. Only in an inequitable, inhumane economic system would there be these incredibly vast differentials in the distribution of wealth. Why not treat the masses compassionately by ensuring they have enough? If one will not do so for the idealistic morality of such a system, then one can do so for the pragmatism of a system that keeps the masses satiated."

I watched the pudgy man behind the counter cut two slices of bread off a loaf and make a sandwich before I considered Sophia's words and replied, "Sophia, we have a name for this distribution argument where I come from. It's called Communism."

A tolerant smile blessed Sophia's face. "As I said, Democratism is not Communism *or* Capitalism, John. The redistribution of wealth that global minimums necessitate and utter emphasis on a democratic power is not the same as either system. Democratism's goal is to ensure that everyone has *enough* and can have the freedom to cultivate sense of self. Our labor commissions and mandatory unionization prevent the abuse of labor by the management, which is a primary factor in many of the abuses and inequities of the past. And our tax system, which I will explain to you soon, makes it possible to provide global minimums to the people while lessening the polarization of wealth that tears apart any Capitalist society. Don't misunderstand me – there are still inequities in our wealth. But the Democratist system ensures that they will not become dangerously vast. It steps around the deep vistas of economic inequality that reign in a Capitalist system that tends to teeter out of control.

"The economic inequality is also negative to the economy as a whole from a pragmatic point of view. How can the economically poor keep contributing more money to the cycle of economic exchange in Capitalism if they don't have any money to give? It's absurd! And yet it occurs over and over again when your Capitalist system is left unchecked. The owners become consumed by greed, and the workers must take it on the chin or lose their jobs. This practice spreads like a disease amongst business owners in the name of almighty unitrade. Without a constant check and balance of the servicement and the peoplement on the businesses to keep the playing field equal and fair, the economy gets to a point where the business owner *must* try to cheat his laborers in order to compete for that almighty prize of unitrade. Eventually, great sums of wealth are piled up amongst the competing wealthy while the sordid masses are left to scrounge for enough. Democratism ends that scrounging of the masses through its use of global minimums, and at the same time, it eliminates the widespread injustice that is lit by the match of the widespread and uneven distribution of wealth. In other words, Amoenians made a conscious and humanitarian choice – it was necessary to trade some economic self-expression to ensure the material well-being of all. It is a moral choice but it is also a practical choice that Amoenians made and continue to make. It is the most compassionate alternative in the eyes of most Amoenians."

I was swishing an ice cube around my mouth. I nodded in agreement, but just as I did, a red flag popped into my mind from my understanding of an entry level book on economics I read some time ago. "That *sounds* great, Sophia. But I know that in economics, one needs to account for incentives. And I am uncertain as to what is the incentive for Amoenian managers – business owners, to invest in progressing *technologically*, you know? I mean, what is in it for them to invest in new equipment so they can make more money and, as a byproduct of making more money, help humanity to progress technologically?"

"Your premise is that technological advancement is produced by competition. But Amoenians have disproved that philosophy. Give the genius of people free time to express themselves and inventions will pour forth like the candy out of a broken piñata. Global minimums give people free time. They eliminate the need for people to spend all their time trying to satiate their basic needs. Therefore, the people – or many of the people – focus their time on much more constructive tasks. They have more time to cultivate their hobbies, talents, and minds. That's why the wonderful and necessary production of art is omnipresent throughout Amoena Vieta. And that's why technological progress will not remain stagnant despite our de-emphasis on competition.

"And as for incentives, unitrade is primarily a status issue under the materialistic handcuffs of Capitalism. But since status and vanity are parts of self-expression, and since people need to cultivate a unique self-image, Amoena Vieta has preserved a small degree of wealth inequity. There are still 'rich' and 'poor' divisions of wealth in Democratism. The difference, though, is that in Democratism, the 'poor' have *enough*, and the wealth of the 'rich' is only limitless so long as the 'poor' have enough. As long as there are differences in wealth, there will be economic incentives for people to have more material wealth than their brothers and sisters."

"That's logical," I said. "But there is one thing that Democratism does not change about Capitalism. And I'm not sure it can be changed, either."

"What's that, John?"

"You haven't eliminated the 'this-for-that,' or, as you called it, 'quid pro quo' that Capitalism is based on. The private sector of your economy still hinges on that ideal."

Sophia stood up in silence, and I became momentarily worried that I'd somehow offended her. She placed a small piece of blue paper on the table. The thin blue paper had a picture of the statue with the shaking hands that I saw on the global servicement building. Then she looked at me and ended the temporary, awkward silence, "Come on John. I'll explain how Democratism deals with quid pro quo in our way. I have more to show you, and there is not much time."

I got up without protesting and began to follow her just as I had before. I remember seeing a few reddish-hued faces looking at me, and I smiled as I walked out of the deli and back onto the path. A brisk, warm breeze caressed us, and Sophia began speaking,

"As I told you before, John, Amoenians generally do not want society to destroy any aspect of what we consider innate human behavior. We understand that society rears and molds human beings, and yet, paradoxically, we also know that human beings create the society that molds them. And we have utilized the tremendous power of the internet to create a world wherein *everyone* does, indeed, have a say in how society should be run. But in all our history books – since the beginning of recorded time – human beings have almost always designed a society governed by an economic system that is either directly or indirectly based on the idea of quid pro quo. From manorialism to feudalism to the simple practice of bartering, from capitalism to communism to socialism, some form of quid pro quo is implicit in every economic system ever designed. Capitalism is a person-to-person quid pro quo exchange. Communism is the person to servicement 'this for that' exchange. The aspect that is common to both is the idea of trading 'this for that.' It is virtually unavoidable for self-interested beings that we are to avoid the practice of quid pro quo. And it would be a foolish, vain, self-destructive practice to ignore this fact. Much of our thought is guided by self-interest, and quid pro quo is similarly guided by a form of reciprocal self-interest. Quid pro quo, then, is both sensible and rational. That, of course, does not make it a good or right or a just practice – only an unavoidable one for human beings.

"We differ from Adam Smith's viewpoint in the actual *cultivation* of quid pro quo in human beings. It exists – that is undeniable. But that doesn't mean we have to build a system that cultivates it. Quid pro quo acts like a leech on the skin of human relations, drawing selfish motives to the surface. Things like patronage cannot substitute for conversation and affection. Materialism cannot replace human contact. This very natural human instinct of reciprocity – of quid pro quo – was identified and cultivated and an economic system was built around it. Amoenians disagree that this should be the order of things. An economic system that cultivates quid pro quo makes people think of people as a means to an end rather than an end in themselves."

"*Agreed* Sophia," I said as I looked down a long, winding road, "I agree that quid pro quo is not the ideal concept upon which to base an economic system. But *how* do you – I mean Amoena Vieta – *how* does it minimize this unavoidable practice?"

"We cut its dehumanizing effect in half by providing a safety net and, therefore, eliminating physiological and material *needs* among the people. We have found that the desire to satiate these basic human needs – when left unchecked – is partially responsible for turning human beings into greedy,

selfish, quid pro quo obsessed creatures. The economic safety net that Democratism provides for the
people eliminates the worry about satiating need
and allows humankind to focus on higher strata of
thought, such as self-actualization and meaning.
This is primarily why art is so prized and produced
throughout Amoena Vieta. Art is the material product of humanity's search for meaning in their lives.

"But you are right. The fact remains that a large
sect of every peoplement's economy – the private
business sect – is based on the quid pro quo ideal.
However, unlike Capitalist economic systems implemented in the past, Amoenian Democratism does
not let quid pro quo run amok amongst our citizenry.
The Capitalist concept of using people for material
gain is still present in our society – make no mistake
about that, John. But it is discouraged immensely by
our culture. And so long as we have taken the precautions we have taken, the 'this-for-that' philosophy
cannot destroy the humanity of our citizens. If we did
not institute these safeguards against the influence of
materialistic quid pro quo, society would inevitably
devolve as it has in past societies. One need only look
into the history books to see the social chaos, the
inhumanity that unregulated Capitalism produced
in every country where it stands, not to mention the
utter instability of the system itself. And wherever
material quid pro quo reigns without the necessary

safeguards installed to combat its dehumanizing effects on the people, there cannot be a true commonweal. There cannot be a truly beneficent society that provides for all its members."

"Okay," I said, "so, you de-emphasize quid pro quo through culture and provide a material safety net to ensure that people won't become inhumane toward people in order to satisfy their basic physiological needs. It seems like it would work if it could be done."

"It can be done, John. The only thing that limits the progress of society is the unwillingness of human beings within that society. There will never be complete agreement on any issue that deals with the commonweal. And that is a wonderful thing – it demonstrates the diversity of views that human beings have. The key is constant compromise and a willingness to work with each other for the betterment of all. These are the hallmarks of society. And it can be accomplished. Society must never stop working together to improve itself."

I nodded, and we continued walking side by side along the path, listening to the crunch of gravel underneath our feet with each step. Sophia directed us in the opposite direction from which we came. Of course, I had no idea where she was taking me.

Sophia pointed straight ahead of us. In the distance, I saw she was pointing to a large, square building. I squinted, and on the top, I could just make out a large statue in the shape of a rectangle. As we came closer, I saw it was a large, white marble statue of a book.

"What is it?" I asked.

Sophia spoke without hesitation. As she turned toward me, the sunlight flashed off her brilliant green eyes, "It's a school. Any true commonweal *must* educate its citizens as best it can. Education is the wellspring of culture, and culture is the wellspring of the commonweal. It is within the walls of our schools that quid pro quo and other thought processes that can be harmful are lessened exponentially. It is there that *service* to others is taught as the *greatest* means of exchange one can use."

CHAPTER 5

EDUCATION

We drew closer to the building, and as we walked, I saw the transport weave around a nearby hill. The grass was green and especially well-kept where the path passed by the large building.

As we approached the building, I saw that it was not the same size as any other I'd seen in the local peoplements of Amoena Vieta. It was only a little taller than the others were, but it was *much* deeper, sort of like the global and local peoplement buildings. When we came closer, I could see that it was really two regular-sized buildings made into one. There was a small, almost imperceptible distance between the two buildings so that it appeared like one giant building. The entire education building was bright white in color. The stone that composed its surface was very similar to the global servicement building's composition. Once I was close enough, I could read the single word that was chiseled onto the cover of the enormous statues of a book that stood atop the building. It read, "Saggezza." As soon as I could make the word out, I pointed and turned and asked Sophia,

"What does Saggezza mean?"

"It is Italian for 'wisdom.' Each peoplement has to, by global decree, have a building similar to this one that not only serves as a conduit for knowledge, but as a conscious cultivator of wisdom. Let's go in."

I followed her into the school, and as I entered, I saw the door was adorned by laurel leaves carved out of a green marble that contrasted very well with the white marble of the building. I couldn't resist but reach out and let my hand glide across the cool, smooth marble of the building as I entered.

I immediately heard the soft hum of voices resonating in a mix of languages I could not understand. At the place we entered, there was a large room which led to a long corridor. The room was wide and open and plain. It gave off a serious feeling. The only articles that adorned the walls were shelves of books and a large blackboard with handwriting scribbled on it with the word "Avisos" printed in large letters above all the lines of handwriting.

Sophia did not speak but just began walking down the corridor. I followed her and saw a plethora of doors that ran along either side of the hallway. I remember one room emanating the most delicious smell in the world – something like hot apple pie with cinnamon. But Sophia did not take me into that one.

On the walls between the rooms were myriads of very beautiful murals. And I'm telling you, every single one of those murals looked as beautiful as pieces by Monet or Picasso or any of the greats! I mean, I know art is subjective and all, but these paintings were done in such a way as to vibrate my very soul. They were so beautiful – painted in such a variety of different colors – each of which seemed to be the perfect hue for the painting. Most of the muses for the paintings were regular things. There were two people throwing a ball in one, and a boy and a girl hugging each other – nice images, you know? The hall had about thirty rooms or so and I looked at each mural like it was a masterpiece, because, to me, each one was. And they were all done in such a variety of different styles, too. Some were impressionistic, some abstract, and still others were as realistic as reality. I touched a few paintings and ran my finger along the upraised paint as if trying to mimic the genius of the person who had painted it.

We came to the end of the hall, and there was a glass door, a little room, another glass door, and then another hall. Before Sophia opened the second glass door, she began to speak.

"Amoenians generally believe that the true measure of the justness of any society is how it disperses resources and treats the least or poorest amongst them. As you have seen, poverty in Amoena Vieta is only a relative term. It is virtually a thing of the past in the sense you know the word.

"But both the quality and longevity of a society do not rest solely in the economic system or social structure. We believe the true measure of the longevity of society, and the measure of enlightenment that keeps the river of democracy flowing through a commonweal, is education. Education is likely to pull out of humanity that strain of goodness that beats at its core. It is what forms the bedrock of a society's culture. It also gives people the ability to think about that knowledge in a critical way that is imperative for democracy to function optimally. Education is so important in Amoena Vieta that we consider it a basic necessity – a global minimum. Every good and just society in the past has empowered the populous through education, and Amoena Vieta is no exception to that rule. It is a staple of life and, perhaps, *the* most important system that human beings create to fuel a well-functioning democracy."

I nodded and ran my hand along the smooth glass door. I felt a little of my claustrophobia kick up as we stood between the two glass doors, and I didn't want to have a long, drawn-out conversation while my blood pressure was surging. Sophia seemed to sense my eagerness, and we promptly walked out the other glass door and into the second hall. I felt more comfortable and began speaking,

"I couldn't agree much more about education, Sophia. Is this where the younger kids go to school or where the older kids go?"

"Both are here. There are sections – rooms – for younger children and sections for older children. And there are also rooms reserved for young adults and rooms reserved for older adults."

"Adults?' I said surprisedly. "Oh, you must mean the folks who fail over and over. I knew a bunch of them in my –"

"No. I mean adults who have completed their rudimentary schooling but continue to yearn for knowledge or, as often is the case, yearn for the opportunity to advance their vocation. You will find these adults in the education centers of every peoplement throughout Amoena Vieta. The way each peoplement administers education may be different, but the education itself – the setup of the system – is by global law since it is included in Eternal Rights."

As she spoke, we walked down the second corridor. The rooms, the walls, and the dimensions were virtually a replica of those in the first hall. The murals were just as beautiful but were more adult in theme. For instance, one had a picture of a couple eating and another with a couple embracing, and there were others with people who were clearly hurt – blood and all – with other people mending their wounds.

"You see," Sophia continued, "Amoenians believe the education of a human being never ends. And we recognize the education of the members of a society unavoidably leads to the enrichment of that society. It is a general rule that as the education level is raised in a human being, the cruelty level tends to be lowered. Education, then, is like an elixir that oftentimes brings out the higher moral road of humankind. And so, since education is both necessary for the individual members of a society and, since it is also good for the commonwealth of society, education is a public good at all levels.

"We just left the section of the education building reserved for the rudimentary school. Rudimentary school is required for all citizens. It is where the *basics* are learned," she said with her thumb leveled like a hitchhiker's to indicate that where we just came from was where the rudimentary school was held. "Reading and writing, math, science, and history are all taught there, and each Amoenian is given a sampling of other disciplines and philosophies. After rudimentary school is completed, courses are offered constantly in a wide variety of disciplines, cultivating skills and conveying information that can be used for the creation of public and private goods or for personal fulfillment. This learning is called extended education. The keystone philosophy of our optional extended education is that knowledge should be readily available to cultivate oneself without the burden of expense. In other words, our education system is based on the idea that uni-trade should not bar any individual from the fruits of higher learning. This is in direct contradiction to most old societies. They treated knowledge and information as if it were a private commodity only accessible for the benefit of wealthy minds. But I ask you, what fairness is in that, John? Should only those able to pay have the opportunity to improve themselves with blessed knowledge? It is education that has the capacity to cultivate the goodness of humankind and polish the pearl of humanity within them all. Should only the materially strong receive this? We in Amoena Vieta believe that since limitless education is a necessity for the well-being of both the individual and the whole, it should be a public good – freely accessible to all willing minds for their own enrichment."

"But what if most people choose the same extensive education field to study? Then you are left with a great deal of the 700 in each peoplement in one discipline and next to none in the others. And that'll send the peoplement's economy tumbling down upon itself, won't it? Unless the peoplement tells everybody what they must study…"

Sophia brushed a strand of hair behind her ear, "Nothing like that need ever occur. For the servicement to order anyone to occupy an economic position against their will – aside from the two years of service to the commonweal – would be a direct infringement on the eternal right of self-expression. So long as human beings are human beings, there will be tremendous variation between their personal likes and dislikes. There is no problem with the allocation of labor or education due to three factors. The first is the general and eternally visible rule of the human diversity of preferences. People choose to fill different vocations, and this truth is the first protection against all people picking the same discipline or career choice. The second deals with market laws of the private sector. In the private sector, there will never be an overload of individuals in one discipline due to natural, free market forces. A surplus of labor and skill to any sect of the private sphere would be inherently self-defeating since a surplus of labor translates into a surplus of competition in the market. A surplus of competition in the market would diminish profit. A diminished profit generally leads to less incentive. Despite the fact that Amoenian culture disapproves of the personal accumulation of wealth, there are some who still pursue material excess. Therefore, it would be against many Amoenian's interests to all flock to the same classes in our educational system in their preparation for the private sector. The third factor that ensures a relatively even distribution of education and vocation is the uses of benefits and sanctions. The needs of the people, which are determined by their vote for global minimums and local minimums, also determine the benefits allotted to entice one to a certain profession. In other words, if a peoplement needs more people educated in water purification if the demand exceeds the supply of labor, the peoplement will add certain benefits to the water purification worker contract – until the need is met. This still ensures people's freedom to choose vocations and ensures that the needs of the people are met in each peoplement. Understand?"

"Sure."

"Good," she said as she motioned toward one of the rooms in the long corridor we were walking, "Let me show you the inside of one of the extensive education rooms." She immediately knocked twice on the thin wooden door of the room, and it slid open. I followed Sophia into the room. The first thing I noticed was the line of computers across the back wall of the room. There were enough to

meet the needs of each of the fifteen to twenty people I saw there. All but one sat at desks made of the
same white marble as the statues on the buildings
throughout Amoena Vieta. The other person sat at
a desk in the front of the room, and when my gaze
reached her, I saw she was looking at me. She had
blonde, curly hair and an upturned nose. I thought
she was very pretty.

After I broke the locked gaze between the woman
in the front and me, I looked over at the fifteen people at the desks. Each one of their bodies was turned
around in their seat, and each face was turned in our
direction. I looked over the sea of blue and brown
and green eyes that sought my own. The fifteen
people were obviously adults, and their ages were
so varied I'd be hard-pressed to say an average age. I
stood next to Sophia quietly, and there was an awkward silence that seemed to permeate the room like
poisonous gas. Finally, Sophia pointed toward me as
she looked at the young blonde woman in the front.
The blonde woman nodded toward Sophia, and a
few moments later, she spoke in a high, demanding
voice, "Nevermind ellos," and all the heads in front
of me turned toward her. The woman stood up and
began talking, and before long, I felt like Sophia
and I were invisible. I remember feeling like I was
Scrooge and Sophia was one of the ghosts from *A
Christmas Carol*. No one took any notice of us, and

it was just as if we were invisible spirits for the rest of the time we were there.

"What are they learning in here?" I asked. Before she answered, I glanced around the room. It was large and square, and the walls were painted a light blue color. On the back wall where the computers were, there was a bay window that stretched most of the wall's length and gave the room a light, airy, open feeling. The bay window presented a view of the path that Sophia and I were walking down just before we came in. Panes of the window were opened slightly to let the air of the beautiful day come inside. I could feel a wisp of warm air caress my face every now and then. Each gust of air brought with it an intoxicating smell of some flower or plant that I could not name. The bay window ran alongside the building – and the side of the building served as the back of the room. I guess they set up the classrooms that way on purpose so that all the students would only be looking out the windows when they were on the computers. Otherwise, their backs were toward the window.

Murals were painted on top of the blue background of the wall. I recognized some as portraits of famous authors: Whitman and Steinbeck, Dickens and Shakespeare, Virgil and Sophocles. Others were of writers I didn't know. But they were all as beautiful and as lifelike as could be.

"This is an extensive learning room for literature, John. The people in front of you are from the peoplement we have been in – they are either here because they are thirsty for knowledge or because they want to write as a career," she said as she looked at the back row of the shoulders of the students. "See the books on their desks?"

I took a step or two forward so that I could see over the shoulder of one of the students. On his desk was a mound of books, mostly by authors I did not recognize and titles I could not understand. But there were two books I did recognize. One was Orwell's *1984*, and the other was *Utopia* by Thomas More.

"This course will be offered for a short period, and then another in the realm of literature will replace it. People in the peoplement will join and leave the courses at their leisure, acquiring knowledge and new literary skills all the time."

"That sounds wonderful," I said honestly. "And they really teach all kinds of courses in all kinds of disciplines – just like this? Sort of like, community courses?"

"That's exactly what they are – community courses. Except they are for anyone in the community instead of solely those with the means. Of course, one has to attend the courses – making almost all the classes and doing all the work assigned

– in order to get formal credit for completing it. Formal credit is typically desired when you are trying to show an employer that you are qualified.

"And this," she pointed to the row of shoulders and the blonde woman in the front, "the extensive education of a peoplement's citizens, does wonders for the commonweal in countless ways. Literature is but one way – albeit a very important way of encouraging people to become more humane and communicate with one another. Amoenians who are not getting extensive education for their vocation often enroll in art and literature extensive education courses more than any other. Art and literature serve pivotal roles in our commonweal."

"How so?" I asked as I inhaled another deep breath of a flowery fragrance I could not name.

"Art and literature connect people's experiences and viewpoints. The mutual cohesion between people – the *empathy* that is so often advanced in human beings by the noble pursuit of art and literature – is an essential component for society to feel connected. In other words, the empathy art and literature create is the oil in the engine of a commonweal. Art and literature, unlike any other disciplines, have the unique capacity to teach sweetly, that is, to inform while entertaining. Amoenians recognize this capacity, and many try to produce art. And since

Amoenians do not need to depend on and fight each other for the scraps that the upper classes of Capitalism drop, they have more time to think – to write – to create. Such activities are invaluable to the well-being of any peoplement. Art and literature are self-expression. Self-expression is the illumination of the soul. The illumination of one person's soul can serve as a beacon – a connector – for the souls of others. Thus, art and literature are means by which a connection may be formed between people. There are others – simple palaver – small talk, for instance. And there are extensive education courses offered in that as well. Any subject that constructively connects people – brings them together for something other than hate and divisiveness – is taught, encouraged, and cultivated. Let me contradict a poet you are no doubt familiar with, Robert Frost, in making my point. Amoenians believe that good fences *do not* make good neighbors. And part of our education, then, is geared toward connecting individuals so that humanity can be more unionized for the good of all. It is only due to Democratism's safety net that we are able to offer these opportunities to humanity. It is only due to Democratism that the beauty and goodness of art flourishes in Amoena Vieta with the effect of helping all to be more humane and more compassionate."

I nodded and turned to glance out the back window. For the first time, I think I realized the power and importance of the arts in our lives. The more I thought about all of it afterward, the more I realized it. Sophia was right. From conception until death, art is one means by which we empathize and relate to one another. And it's also one of the cultivators and refiners of our morality, too. Sophia left that out, but the more I think about it, the more I realize it's true. We refine our ideas of right and wrong through stories, nursery rhymes, and religion, which is most often another version of stories.

Sophia nodded to the woman who was speaking in front of the room, and the woman nodded back. Sophia reached down and grabbed my hand, and we walked out of the room together. Once we were out in the hall with the many rooms, she turned and took a long look up and down the hall as if she were an architect surveying the scene. After a few moments, she pointed to the rooms on either side of the room we had just left.

"In these rooms, and maybe others, I'm not sure how this peoplement is set up, but there will be all kinds of art and literature classes offered. Sculpture, poetry, literary movements, and music will be just a few. Each class gives a short history of the art form and then teaches the basics of performing it. We consider it very important to learn the history of the art form, and it is included in every class. That is, we consider the movements and means by which our past family expressed themselves, and we, too, can essentially build on their modes of expression. Learning the artistic and historical movements connects us to our brothers and sisters from the past and simultaneously teaches us different modes of self-expression."

I smiled in awe of such an education system.

"I think you are beginning to understand our extensive education system now. But you must understand that all this is merely optional for Amoenians. Rudimentary education is the only education that is mandatory in all local peoplements. Come with me, and I'll show you what rudimentary education consists of. It is back from where we came," she said before pointing toward the hallway we walked through once we first entered the building, "– the rudimentary education is in the front of the building. I wanted you to see the extensive education first. Let's go," she said as we reached the sets of glass doors that separated the two parts of the education center. Sophia opened the glass door, and we walked through the claustrophobic-inducing little room, the other glass door, and then went back into the rudimentary school hall. My eyes returned to the more child-like pictures that lined the wall, and a scent of lemony wax – the same scent that filled the global servicement – filled the corridor.

* * *

We were in the first corridor where the murals were, the ones I previously saw upon my entrance to the education building. They were beautiful, simple murals, ones of everyday scenes like a man throwing a ball to a boy, a waterfall, a forest, an open field where children were playing... stuff like that. Throughout the hall now wafted a smell different from before. It was... like blueberry muffins or pastries – some sweet confection like that. I turned, and as we walked, I asked Sophia what the smell was.

"It is coming from one of the culinary rooms, John. Food preparation is among the rudimentary Amoenian curriculum. The rudimentary curriculum is part of the education that Amoenians are not only entitled to but are obligated to complete. As I said before, education is the bedrock of a commonwealth. This is where the bare necessities of learning are supplied to all for the good of the individual and society. The subject matter is determined by a global vote every ten years. It is voted on globally so that all children have the same curriculum wherever they are – local peoplements cannot determine which subjects are taught and which aren't. The rudimentary curriculum seldom changes. Language, Literature, Art, Culinary Arts, Psychology, Math, Science, History, Philosophy, Economics, and Ethics or Morality are the eleven major subjects. Rudimentary school is composed of varying levels of these essential disciplines."

She walked casually forward as she spoke, and I followed closely. All the rooms were closed off by a glass door, and as we passed, I peeked into each room and saw many bright-eyed Amoenian children.

"Economics? Ethics?" I questioned, surprised to hear that Amoenian education includes different subjects than those we were taught in grade school and high school.

"The goal of rudimentary Amoenian education is to provide children and adolescents with the essentials of knowledge – the building blocks upon which thought builds itself. The essentials are not solely reading and writing and arithmetic – although that is where it starts. But it is much more than that. It is also teaching them the philosophical archetypes, teaching them compilations or tastes of a wide variety of knowledge. Rudimentary education is also conveying the trials and tribulations of our human predecessors. It is showing what those who came before us came to know as truth through the pain of trial and error and the wonder of observation. Only this can help humans to prevent the negative cycle of history repeating itself. Humankind has always taken two steps forward before taking one step backward. It is through rudimentary education that we are able to take three, four, and five steps forward before taking that dreaded step backward, or, ideally, that we are able to eliminate steps backward altogether."

I nodded.

"And from six years old until eighteen years old, our youth are given these keystones of thought and problem-solving techniques through rudimentary education – year-round. The most well-known psychologists, Freud and Jung, Erikson and Piaget, helped us to understand that the proper education and good learning experiences in these developmental years is essential in enabling the minds of individuals to adequately shape and mold themselves. That is why their rudimentary education is a year-round event," she said before pausing and squinting her eyes as she looked over at me, "but before they can be taught anything, they have to learn bonding and attachment at home, of course. I will discuss their first six years later."

"Okay," I said as I looked up and noticed the halogen-looking lights on the ceiling for the first time. "But I see a contradiction, Sophia," I said boldly. "You say there are morality classes, right?"

"Yes."

"But at the same time one of the Eternal Rights is, 'to thine own self be true,' right?"

"Yes."

"Well, the two aren't compatible. Everyone has, however slightly, a different sense of morality – a different sense of right and wrong. And yet, to be true to oneself would be to follow one's *own* personal morality code, right?"

"Yes, John, but –,"

"Well, then, how can you teach a morality code when everyone's sense of right and wrong is different? What I mean is personal freedom and a specific moral code are, to a large extent, incompatible concepts." When I finished, I was grinning from ear to ear with delight in my own reasoning. I was sure I had her.

But it seemed she was ready for it. She spoke immediately, "You make an excellent observation. But a specific sense of morality – that is – the specific sense of what is right and wrong, good and bad, just and unjust – does not have to stifle personal freedom. Amoenians set what we call a 'baseline' moral code. Other societies called this their 'law code.' But laws and morals cannot be separated. Laws are reflections of the morals of the society that implements them – if that society is a democracy. So, there must be an agreed-upon baseline of morals, yes. That means there must be *some* limit to personal freedom if one is to live by the covenant of a society. But at the same time, Amoenians recognize the importance of

personal freedom and the danger of a stifling universal 'moral' code. That is why we have a 'baseline'
moral code. It is, like all things in Amoena Vieta, a
compromise of viewpoints – a happy medium – an
agreement that satisfies all sides."

"Well, what is it?" I asked impatiently.

"The baseline moral code for our society is
the simple moral principle of no harm. It is the
agreement that whatever life is, for whatever reason we are here, there is one thing we know for
sure. That is that we are all here together and that
we need one another to survive and, more importantly than to survive, to be happy or make meaning. In other words, we are all on the same team.
There must, therefore, be basic rules for us to get
along and play the game of life together. That
basic moral code is the principle of being good to
and not harming others. Almost every great philosophy recognizes this truth. Personal freedom
is limited only to the extent that we honor our
responsibility to others and we do not harm others. After that, we are free to be true to ourselves
in virtually every way."

"So, then, that's all that's taught in morality
class... the moral baseline of being good to and not
harming others?"

"That's all. As we discussed, that is our golden
rule as a society and the formal education in it starts

at six years old. Let me show you," she said and immediately walked to one of the glass doors on the side of the hall. She knocked and motioned to someone in the room. Moments later, the glass door slid open, and Sophia and I entered.

The first thing I noticed in the classroom was the computers. Computers lined every wall. In front of each of the bright computer screens was the oval shape of a little Amoenian head. But the children were not facing the computer. Every single chair was pointed toward the middle of the room, where a tall, heavier-set, brown-haired woman stood. I could see the children's chairs were on swivels so they could face the computers if need be.

The woman in the front quickly spoke, and one by one, the eyes of the students turned away from us and gravitated back to the woman. I looked around the square room and saw more murals covering the walls that looked like they were painted by a child's hand. There was a large, flat-screened television hung from the ceiling that reminded me a little of the one in the global servicement room. That's what the children were mainly looking at when I followed their eyes. On the floor underneath the screen was where the tall, brown-haired woman stood. There was a little computer screen on a podium in front of her, and as she spoke in Amoenish, she drew on and touched the computer screen with her finger. I realized before Sophia said a word that the woman was the teacher, and what she drew on the computer screen was what would appear on the big screen the children watched. The spectacle of the teacher drawing on the screen reminded me of the way the coach of a football team draws up plays. Every so often, from the overhead screen, I heard noises – beeps and other sound effects. They were followed by large, white-toothed smiles on many of the faces of the children.

"This is a rudimentary school class, John."

I pointed to all the screens – behind the students and to the big one above us, and I said, "They make good use of computers, I see."

Sophia smiled, "Yes, we do... for everything. Computers are our best tools for self-expression and self-expression must always be cultivated in a commonweal. The internet is, in fact, one of the primary modes of self-expression. From age six until death, computers are necessary as a driving skill from where you come from. People are taught early and often about computers throughout their lives. Because computers are so necessary, they are the material connection of human beings to one another."

I nodded and continued looking around the square room. All the while I could hear the teacher's voice as she taught the children in a language I could not understand. In front of the room, above a mural picture, I recognized an image that looked like a group of philosophers in white robes sitting around a pond. There, I saw a group of words written in what looked like stencils.

"What is that, Sophia?" I asked as I pointed to the writing that looked Greek to me.

"Those are humanist moral teaching extracts from many of the world's great philosophers and thinkers. You see, this is a morality class. Those," she pointed to the stenciled words, "are the bases of Amoenians and humanistic morality."

"What extracts?" I asked with mounting curiosity. "Could you read them to me?"

Sophia shook her head, "We don't have time to read all of them. But I'll give you a good idea of what they say. At the top is Christianity's 'Love one another,' since there is no better or more definitive humanist statement than that contained in those words. Christianity's Parable of the Good Samaritan and Golden Rule are also there, as well as portions of the Beatitudes.

"Judaism's Commandments that deal with human beings are there because they, too, have been deemed by Amoenians to be wonderful humanistic thoughts. Honor your parents, do not kill, do not commit adultery, do not steal, and do not lie; these are all among the humanist statements of Jewish descent. Islam's Zakat – meaning alms to the poor as well as Islam's emphasis on honoring parents and its belief in being just in one's words, are written there. Hinduism's ideal of treating all living creatures with compassion and the idea of Brahman or greater soul of which we are unified, is also included among the moral teachings Amoenian children learn. Native American and Eastern philosophical humanistic commandments including such as showing great respect for your fellow beings, working together for the benefit of humankind, giving assistance and kindness whenever needed, doing what you know to be right, which, of course, is a paraphrase of to thine own self be true, are all included. These and many others emphasize the dedication to share your efforts for the greater good. It is also illustrated on the wall there, teaching our youth a humanistic compassion that composes a baseline of the Amoenian moral codes.

"And of course, many of Buddhism's Noble Eightfold Path tenants are also listed under our humanist or human-loving baseline of morality that most Amoenians come to accept on some level. Right resolve or goodwill in thought, right speech or speaking kindly, without lies, right conduct or caring actions without harm, and right livelihood or earning a living without harming others, and right effort or working hard to do good are all among the Buddhist moral teachings you see on the wall in front of us. There are the words of an American you are probably familiar with – Ralph Waldo Emerson – and notes from his writings on the idea of an Oversoul," she said, and her eyes continued to scan the wall, "Excerpts from Gandhi's writings, phrases by Whitman, and other humanist thoughts by thinkers such as Leo Tolstoy or Pico de Mirandella all have excerpts from their writings written on the wall of humanist thought and are contained within every morality classroom. Please understand, John that this is not an attempt of the state to impose morality on the people. These moral teachings form the basis of our legal system. Law and a baseline morality are closely intertwined in Amoena Vieta. After Amoenians learn and ingest these broad baselines of morality – they are free to do whatever their bodies or hearts or minds desire.

"Furthermore, none of these baselines are in stone. No rule or belief system is irrevocable. The people need only to unify and vote in a very high consensus to revoke a rule or general guiding belief system. The general sentiment of loving one's neighbor that runs throughout most religions and all humanist thought is what is taught in morality classes. It is almost indisputably the moral code that is most conducive to a humane society. But suppose an Amoenian's nature compels them to believe our humanist moral baseline is incorrect. In that case, they are free to depart from and abandon it. Because remember, John, to thine own self they must be true. They are always free to embrace and discuss any belief they have. They are also free to challenge the majority."

I looked over the foreign languages that were written on the wall. I was shocked that what seemed like a nonsensical hodgepodge of letters and characters conveyed all that Sophia described: and more. But it was then – even more so than when I was in the community center – that I saw abundance of similarities and links that pervaded the humanistic aspects of morality in all the major religions and amongst the great thinkers and writers who have risen to prominence throughout the ages.

As I pondered my epiphany, I looked back at the seemingly kind-hearted woman who taught the class. All of the faces of the children were set with interest, and I could see they were all using something that looked like a little stick to write whatever the woman was dictating to them. The Amoenian children looked so interested that I could not help but ask Sophia what the teacher was telling them.

Sophia turned from facing the front wall and listened intently for a few moments. She nodded several times as she listened before turning toward me.

"She's teaching a lesson taught by many Amoe-nian philosophers and generally considered to be wisdom in Amoena Vieta. She is teaching that greed and vanity are the roots of inhumanity," Sophia said before turning and waving her left hand to me while pointing toward the door with her right index fin-ger. "But let us go, John. I have more to show you. Come with me," she said and immediately began walking out of the room. I glanced over the rudi-mentary education room one last time to try to freeze the image in my mind. I turned and followed her out into the hall. She motioned toward me, and we walked back through the glass doors and past the extensive education rooms on our way out of the education building.

CHAPTER 6

LEGAL SYSTEM

I inhaled the smell of grass as we entered the beauty that existed everywhere in Amoena Vieta. Sophia walked to the path with me by her side. Neither of us said a word. I was completely engorged in thought by the emphasis Amoenians put on their education. Sophia seemed to understand – and sense – my amazement and just walked silently next to me. Once I heard our footsteps begin clopping off the gravel path, I shook the deep thoughts out of my mind and began to speak,

"Where are you taking me now, Sophia?"

She brushed a bug off her dress and took a deep breath before responding, "I'm going to show you what social life is like for many Amoenians. I am going to give you a taste of the general mores that compose most Amoenian peoplements and tie most Amoenians together by a common culture. You already know about our Eternal Rights, and they are the most important reflection of the shared beliefs we generally have. But there is more to –"

She stopped speaking suddenly and just stared straight ahead. I followed her gaze and saw two men on a slab of pavement just a little way up the road.

They stood on what looked like a basketball or a tennis court that took the place of one of the houses alongside the path. As we both stared, I felt something brush against my leg. I was startled and immediately looked down. It was a squirrel that brushed against me! It was eating some nut I could not recognize, and its long, bushy tail slapped against my pants. I was distracted entirely from the two men. I bent down and put my hand out toward the squirrel to see if it would let me touch its gray, coarse, wiry fur. But the moment I extended my hand, the little animal got frightened. It abandoned the nut at my feet and took off with lightning speed through the grass.

After the furry distraction left, my attention returned to the previously forgotten men. One of the men was large and burly. He had the build we anticipate lumberjacks having. The other man was significantly smaller in stature. He was roughly the size of the majority of the people I saw in Amoena Vieta. The men were talking to one another, and even at a distance, their voices were fairly audible. Of course, I didn't understand any of what they were saying, but still, I could comprehend the tone and the general drift of the conversation. It was obvious they were arguing. Next to where they stood was a circular disk with a bunch of other circles within it. It looked something like frisbee, only there were circles inside the big circles with spaces in between. I stood quietly, listened, and glanced toward Sophia, hoping she would explain what they were saying so that I might understand.

"Just watch, John," she said in reply to my glance. "You need not know exactly what they are saying. You can see they are having an argument. And you can see the argument is quickly escalating. I wasn't planning on revealing to you this aspect of our society until later. But the opportunity has presented itself, and, therefore, I will rearrange the chronology of what I show you accordingly." Her long, slender finger pointed in the direction of the men, and she looked directly into my eyes with her beautiful green irises as she spoke, "Watch as their human nature consumes them."

I watched as if the spectacle of the two men were the last plays in a tie football game. I even tried to limit my blinks. The men continued to argue, and their voices grew louder and louder. Then something else caught my attention. In the houses near the men, I noticed the window drapes moving. They would open and close, the people in the houses seeing the escalating fight, and then dropping the curtains, letting them fall back into place.

The yelling escalated and I continued to watch with all the interest of a boy during the formation of a high school fight. The bigger man finally erupted into anger – it didn't take long – and his enormous right arm came around like a human bat. His fist connected with the other man's face, and I heard a hollow smacking sound as it collided with the cheekbone of the little man, sending him staggering backward like a spent boxer in the last rounds of a fight.

Immediately I started toward the two men because, you know, I can't stand to see a little guy like that get beaten up. But I didn't take three steps before I felt Sophia's gentle, warm hand clutching my collar and stopping me in my tracks. I turned and looked at her with a twinge of anger in my eyes.

"Just watch."

"Watch? I can't *watch* that little guy get pummeled. Let me go, Sophia!" I demanded.

But she did not reply in words. Instead, those bright green eyes just looked up at one of the houses on either side of the court. Her head nodded quickly, and her eyes looked at me and then fixated themselves on the house.

I looked where she was looking and saw a skinny, dark-haired lady come running out. She yelled "Luta!" at the top of her lungs, and within no time, the doors of most of the little houses around her flung wide open. Six or seven people came streaming out of their doors. There were at least five men, two women, and two children running frantically toward the two fighting men. I couldn't help but think of a pack of wolves or a hive of bees as they closed almost instantaneously on the man. Every one of them grabbed the large man and pulled him off the diminutive little fellow with both speed and precision. They did not throw the large man off cruelly or violently, but rather like they were a teacher stopping a schoolyard fight. It was then that I could feel Sophia release my collar and we both stood and watched.

The bigger man thrashed violently for a minute while the group held him down – four held an appendage. The others – one portly man and one of the children stood in between the group and the smaller man who was being beaten. The beaten man did not challenge the portly man, though. He sat up on his own and used his white shirt to wipe the dark red blood cascading from his nose. The portly man walked over and helped the beaten man stand up on his feet, and I watched as the beaten man nodded several times, obviously grateful for the assistance.

"What's happening, Sophia?" I asked. I felt the adrenaline and the anger slowly ebbing.

"You are getting a taste of our justice system, John. The citizens are playing out their legal responsibility to be Good Samaritans."

"Legal *responsibility*?" I asked in shock. "You mean they could be legally liable for *not* stopping the fight?"

"As I've alluded to several times, Amoenians have global laws that apply to all local peoplements. Most of the people in Amoena Vieta decided that the Good Samaritan law should be part of the global legal framework. That means that any Amoenian who is able to help another Amoenian in distress using non-violent means is obligated by law to do so. Otherwise, the individual who did not help when she or he could have can be reported to the legal commission of the peoplement."

"Legal commission?"

"They are one of the watchdog groups elected every year in each peoplement. The legal commission is responsible for enforcing the global servicement's laws and whatever laws the local peoplement has instituted for the safety and benefit of the commonweal. The group is generally called the *peacekeeping commission* in each peoplement."

I watched as the large man was helped up by the group who pinned him and I could hear soft murmuring voices as they spoke to the two men. I turned to Sophia,

"Where are the cops?"

She responded as if she expected the inquiry, "Amoenians do not see it necessary to elevate a small sect of the population by granting them physical power over the rest of the population. Humanity's natural tendency to abuse power forbids this practice in a well-functioning, egalitarian society. In Amoena Vieta, the *people* are the cops. They are guided by the Good Samaritan principle. They are guided by the idea that each person has a legal responsibility to help another person if that other person is in trouble. An Amoenian in need has a legal obligation to help another Amoenian in need."

I objected immediately, "But that whole premise is impossible to prove, isn't it? I mean, how could someone prove that someone could have helped a person – but didn't?"

She took a few steps forward on the path and stared off at the group before us as she spoke, "Many times it cannot be proven if there are no witnesses or circumstantial evidence to support an accuser's claim." She turned her head toward me, "No legal system made by human beings – in fact – no *thing* made by human beings has ever been made perfectly, John. This is the best way we have devised thus far, though. Crime is exponentially reduced in Amoena Vieta because of Democratism. This is in stark contrast to the rates of crime that soar under a Capitalist society. Capitalism leaves people fighting over the crumbs left by the invisible hand. Due to material inequity, crime soars. There are many who do not have enough and their needs cause them to engage in negative behaviors. In Amoena Vieta, crime is reduced greatly because these inequities don't exist and the culture is far more humanistic. However, as long as human beings are human beings, crime will occur. We have decided that it is absurd to elevate a group of flawed individuals like the rest of us to act as the enforcers of laws. Many societies of the past place all sorts of restrictions on the power of the police. Even if they are somehow able to implement those restrictions, the fact remains that the police are, without being elected, given far more power than the rest of the individuals in a society. Enforcing those restrictions becomes incredibly difficult. Therefore, we recognize the folly and danger in granting a small portion of the population power over the rest of society. That power will inevitably get abused.

"Therefore, every citizen – every woman, man, and child – has the authority and obligation to help every other man, woman, and child in society. The Good Samaritan law is the foundation of all Amoenian law. And as I said before, Democratism makes it possible."

"What do you mean? What does Democratism – the economic system – have to do with the legal system?"

She adjusted the purple flower that she placed above her ear before responding, "John, did you notice that in every one of those houses, there was at least one person home?"

I had thought nothing of it until Sophia mentioned it. The people who came out to help all came from the surrounding houses. "No," I replied after my observation, "but now that you mention it..."

"Do you find it odd," she went on, "that so many were home in the middle of the day – when you're probably used to seeing people spend most of their time trading in their hours for unitrade?"

"Yeah... that is kind of strange now that you say it. Why *are* so many people home in this," I looked up at the sprawling, sunny, and very blue sky, "in what must be just a little while after the middle of the day?"

"Let me explain. Amoenians recognize that a child's most important developmental years are the child's earliest years. We have learned that it is exponentially more beneficial developmentally if a child is reared surrounded by the most important human qualities: love, compassion, and empathy. We have also learned that those qualities, if dispensed to the child by someone who truly loves her or him, will exhibit positive loving and caring qualities and behaviors. Psychologists, sociologists, and countless other social scientists discovered this truth and we have seen it proven over and over again throughout the ages. That is why Amoenians have voted to institute a global law, that is, a law that has jurisdiction spanning across all local peoplements – stating that until any child reaches a certain age, one parent must be home with him or her. One of the parental figures is the most likely source to provide this love and care due to an instinctual longing to protect and guide their children. Therefore, they are not only expected but obligated to provide that protection and guidance. It is not left to caretakers who care for the child as a vocation and not for honor and privilege."

"When you say the parents must take care of the child, you are saying the mother takes care of the child, right?" I asked impulsively.

Sophia laughed loudly. "Of course not, John! Amoenians would not, like civilizations of the past, breed a culture that robs one sex of their economic freedom and deprives the other of the joy and pains of raising children. It does not matter which parent or caregiver stays with the child during these all-important years. Just so that *one* parent or caregiver does, the child has an infinitely higher chance of receiving the almighty qualities of the love, empathy, and compassion the fuel Amoena Vieta. We leave it up to the parents themselves to determine who will and won't stay home with the child. And if there is only one parent: then yes, she or he *must* give up their economic freedom to stay with the child during those all-important years or find a way for a loving and constant caregiver to nurture the child..."

"For how many years of the child's life?" I asked.

"That's up to the peoplement, John. The number varies. But one parent must be with the child until he or she is at *least* six years old. That is the minimum age that a peoplement can choose. And that minimum age gives the caregiver time to ingrain the love, compassion, and empathy that beats the heart of our community. Global law is also, incidentally, a form of population control as well. Fewer people have children if they know they must stay with the child and actually raise her or him, which, of course, is their choice entirely. The willingness to dedicate those years to the raising of the child is, in a way, a test of parenthood."

I walked alongside her in confusion. "But what about the individual's general right to do whatever he or she wants?" I asked.

Sophia replied instantly. "What is of greater importance, the cultivation of love and empathy in those who will carry the torch of society onward or the right of parents to leave their child to be taken care of by babysitters, daycare employees, and other individuals who can't help, on some level, but view the children as a job? The child, to them, is on some level a means to unitrade. These individuals are talented caregivers. However, the child will be able to detect the underlying motives unconsciously or consciously and it will affect her psychological development.

Her answer was overwhelming. "I see your point, Sophia. I guess when you look at it like that, there's really no contest," I said, and we continued walking along the stone path side by side.

* * *

As we continued walking under the warm sun, I drank in the intoxicating air. Sophia remained quiet as we walked, and I thought about all she said. Questions arose in my mind, and I voiced them.

"Let's go back to the legal system for a minute, Sophia. What happens when a compromise cannot be reached between the community and the offender? And what if there is a *group* of individuals who hurt others and *can't* be stopped by the community?"

She smiled broadly and replied, "Let me answer your second question first. In the event that a gang forms and hurts others in the community, and the community is unable to stop the gang, the elected peacekeeping group is charged with the responsibility of pacifying the unruly group. They are able to use nonviolent pacification tools such as non-harmful gases to quell the gang and, once quelled, detain and rehabilitate them. But in all the history of Amoena Vieta, these means of pacification have been used so sparingly that it is hard to recall even one instance when it has been done. Suppose the peacekeeping group – a group elected to a yearly term – uses its power in any way that is unsatisfactory to the commonweal. In that case, the commonweal may immediately remove the peacekeeping group from office by the majority of votes. As you know, the commonweal always has this power with every elected leader in the land. The power of the vote is the true power in a democratic state. The true power in the state of Amoena Vieta is always in the hands of the citizens."

While Sophia spoke, one of the most delectable scents I have ever had the good fortune to smell drifted into my nose. It smelled like some fresh, delicious fruit. I looked around for the origin of the blessed smell and my nose led me like an olfactory detective to the general direction of the houses that lined the right side of the path. I continued to take long, deep breaths so the deliciousness could saturate my lungs and make my mouth water like a pool filled with water. As we passed the house, Sophia answered the other half of my question.

"Now insofar as uncompromising cases are concerned, that is, cases that cannot be remedied through reason by the parties involved – they are settled by a neutral and well-educated third party."

"You mean a judge?" I said impulsively.

"Not exactly. Not in the way I think you conceive of a judge. In Amoena Vieta, we have employed all barriers to stop corruption in our legal system. You see, corruption has reigned in legal systems since the dawn of civilization. There are three basic cogs that history has shown are necessary to remove from the wheels of justice. The first is unitrade. There is no unitrade in our legal system just as there is none in our politics. This is based on the principle that unitrade injects a stick in the spokes of justice. It ruins the fairness of almost all societal institutions of which it is a part.

"But its elimination is not enough to keep the wheel of justice rolling smoothly. Amoenians also had to find a way to remove the other sticks in the spokes of justice. More specifically, we had to remove nepotism and cronyism from the process.

"Our versions of judges live honorable but secluded lives. They live away from much of the world. They are philosophers, and they are students of humanity. The philosophical and practical study of humanity is required by their office. They do not, however, have to know the arduous and erroneous details of countless law books. The only laws are the Eternal Rights and the overarching law that states we must love our brothers and sisters. There is nothing more to criminal law than this. One is generally free to do whatever she or he wants to her or himself. Only actions that are to the direct detriment of others are prohibited. If a case reaches the judge, what the judge decides goes and is enforceable by the peacekeepers. That is why most conflicts are mediated by the two groups through almighty compromise.

"There are no courts or customs that have surrounded the judges of the past. If two parties cannot resolve their conflict and, therefore, must take it to a mediator, or judge, each party states their case to the best of their ability, and the judge decides whose case is more reasonable. The judge must, of course, provide ample reasoning for why she or he believes it is the more reasonable side."

"Excuse me, Sophia," I said as we passed a large, square pine board nailed to a post. The board was wide – a few feet across. I ran my finger along its coarse exterior and got a small splinter in my finger. I noticed the wooden board had papers pinned to it that were written in Amoenish. I pulled the sliver out of my finger and continued, "I didn't want to interrupt your explanation of the legal system, but I can't help it. What is this?" I pointed to the board with my slightly wounded finger.

"That's called the community board. Citizens can freely post whatever they choose on it for all to

see. The only prerequisite for posting is that its subject matter must pertain to organizing members of
the community – in other words, meetings. It's a way
for the community to cultivate their interests with
one another and has proven to be remarkably beneficial to the commonweal. It is another safeguard we
use to prevent the disassociation of the community
– to encourage unity." She squinted at the board,
"There is everything from religious meetings to
meetings for pet lovers to sports leagues on it. Any
common interest may be listed."

I nodded, and we continued to walk. I saw a
treatment center with a large marble statue of a
human brain gracing its roof. For the first time, I
didn't have to consult Sophia. I realized that it was a
mental health treatment center almost immediately.
As we passed it, I urged Sophia to continue our discussion about the legal system.

"The judge listens to each side and asks questions
from both parties. After that, the judge retires to her
or his seclusion, where the case is pondered, and a
ruling is decided. Of course, no judge is allowed to
rule on any case involving a spouse or someone she or
he is close to in any way – especially a blood relation.
Although Amoenians cultivate a feeling of and generally see themselves as one large family, it is impossible to eradicate nepotism altogether. That is why
judges – the interpreters of our laws – live in relative

seclusion, wherein it is not easy to be influenced by corrupting forces of any sort. It is a respected and noble position that requires limited influence from the outside world. Judges are required leave behind most of their social connections in the name of objectivity toward the commonweal. No one is able to contact or influence a judge. They take a vow of segregation so that they can focus only on their work of interpreting the law. This is the only way to prevent unfair influence by any party."

"I see – they're sort of like Christian monks."

"I guess you could say that. There is a purpose that judges are in relative seclusion just as there is a purpose that monks are. It provides a sort of... purification from bias."

"You said that each citizen makes their own argument before the judge – if the case reaches a judge – right?"

"Yes," she said and nodded.

"So, then, there are no lawyers to make arguments for the people?"

"No," she paused and looked in the air thoughtfully before adding, "not exactly."

"What do you mean – not exactly?"

"Well John, not all individuals can argue their case equally well – which I think was where you were going with that line of questioning, right?"

I nodded.

"So, then, you would be right to point out that a justice system based on the ability of each defendant and prosecutor to make a good argument is, inherently, biased against those who have not been given talents in art of arguing and debate. And a legal system that favors the better debater is not a great deal better than, say, a legal system based on who has the most money and therefore prejudiced against the 'poor' – one which I am sure you know all too well."

She smiled and I nodded and smiled back in agreement.

"We have anticipated and attempted to remedy that flaw by supplying 'counselors.' Counselors are schooled in the art of debate. The commonwealth supplies every defendant and prosecutor with a counselor."

"Isn't the counselor just a lawyer?"

Sophia smiled and exhaled, "A lawyer's job is not only to produce arguments but also to present them, right?"

"Well, yes."

"And don't lawyers get paid – often by private citizens – as if to suggest justice has a price and can be bought?"

"Yeah, that's true."

"And don't lawyers sometimes have a personal relationship with the judge to whom they present the case?"

"I've heard that."

"Then you see the answer to your question is 'no.' A counselor is an argument creator or dismantler. They are a suggestion maker. Nothing more."

By this time, we had made it down the road, past what I was sure was the mental health treatment center. In the middle of one of the rows of houses was a structure that looked like a wide, grey warehouse. I could smell something like the smell of grass invading the sweet air as we passed. Behind the warehouse lay a gigantic pole with a wheel of large, sprawling metal blades attached to it. It looked like an enormous pinwheel. When I asked Sophia, she said it was a windmill and that it – along with solar power – was how Amoenians produced electricity. She noted the idiocy of other civilizations that split the uranium atom to produce one of the deadliest substances the earth has ever known, plutonium, to produce electricity. She said this way was infinitely more wise and constructive. After the interlude, she continued,

"The Amoenian legal system's keystones are its understandability, accessibility, and its simplistic laws. It is manageable and has the ability to place the power of law in the people's – and not the authority's – hands. Because always remember, John, the judges are elected. They are beholden to the people and can be removed at any time – like all other elected leaders in Amoena Vieta."

I grinned, "Yes, I have noticed all those facets of your system. Some of them are, in my view, preferable to the justice system I've known. But you have not given me the last piece of the snapshot of your legal system."

"What's that?"

"The punish –" I began to say but stopped as the technical term came to my mind, "the corrections part of the system."

"Ah, I see. I think you were closer to the reality of the system you spoke about when you said punishment. In our experience, 'corrections' is merely a euphemism for punishment. Here, we call the system what it is. We have a rehabilitation system."

I watched and listened as the transport emerged from out of nowhere and sped behind some of the treatment centers we passed. I decided to say nothing and let the silence urge Sophia to elaborate. It wasn't long before she did.

"Amoenians generally believe a true commonweal concerns itself with its members' well-being – the *common wealth*. We believe in the well-being of even those who defy our social contract. We believe a society can be best analyzed by how it treats the least among them – the least economically *and* morally speaking."

"But, Sophia," I automatically said in protest, unable to suppress my rising objection, "are you trying to say that Amoenians coddle their criminals like criminals are some kind of children? Is this what they call justice?"

Sophia looked at me, and I saw something like sympathy flash in her eyes. The look made me angry and only encouraged me to argue the veracity of my point.

"No, John, that is not what we do at all. You must let me explain before you jump to conclusions and criticize. After I explain, I welcome all manner of criticism. It is obvious you feel strongly about the issue. Perhaps something you say can change Amoena Vieta for the better. I will take all you say into consideration."

I calmed down and nodded in agreement. "I'm sorry. Go on."

She bent over and picked up a small, black rock. She turned and looked at each side of it before tossing the rock back onto the path behind us and speaking,

"Let me answer your questions with questions. It seems that your strong objections are founded on philosophical grounds concerning how those who hurt others should be treated. So, I ask you, how would you treat them?"

"It depends on the crime," I answered without hesitation.

"Okay. Theft."

"Jail."

"And by jail, you mean the criminal is removed from mainstream society and put into a society composed of other individuals who have harmed others – by theft or by other means?"

"Yes."

"And in that new society – that of prisons and jails, what occurs? They do not learn how to be productive members of society, do they? Are they taught a trade or made to work? Or are they simply given an education from the other criminals around them – an education that usually consists primarily of learning to be a better criminal?"

"Well, no. That's not how it's supposed to be," I protested. But my thoughts immediately wandered to my cousin. "My cousin's been a prison guard for twenty-five years. He'd worked at every level of the prison system. And that's *exactly* how he says it is in local, state, and federal prisons – except for super-maximum-security prisons, where they keep inmates in solitary all the time."

"But that's not how it is supposed to be, right?" Sophia pressed me.

"Well, no, of course not."

"How, then, is it *supposed* to be, John?" She asked, and a cool wind brushed my face as she spoke.

"Well... it's *supposed* to 'correct' the criminals – that is – teach them that what they were doing was wrong in an attempt to get them to stop doing it."

"Ahhh, now we're getting somewhere," Sophia said with a triumphant, attractive smile that stretched across her face. "Tell me, does fighting fire with fire put out a flame?"

"No."

"Then does countering violence with violence stop people from hurting each other in the long run?"

I thought a moment before replying, "No."

"Do you agree, then, that taking an eye for an eye and a tooth for a tooth just creates a whole world of blind, toothless people?"

"Yeah... I guess so."

"So, then, do you agree that two wrongs do not make a right? Isn't it clear that the commonwealth has the responsibility not to continue the cycle of maltreatment by harming the morally sick through either the physical violence of the baton or the mental violence resulting from putting the morally sick amidst other individuals who are morally sick in a cage? To make matters worse, doesn't it often become a cage where they only teach one another tricks to avoid getting caught the next time?"

I kicked a few stones in frustration because something deep down in me knew she was right. "I see your point, Sophia."

"Are you sure? There are still some Amoenians who believe as you do. Feel free to defend your position!"

"No, Sophia, the more I think about it, I have no position. I guess all I'm really repeating are the stock lines of my culture. Now that I'm actually *thinking* about it, I believe that our practices might not be the best way to go about it. How are we supposed to pick people up and stop them from living in a negative way if we are only removing them from one traumatic environment and placing them into another?"

Sophia grinned the way a mother grins when her child gets the right answer to a tough question. "I could not agree with you more, John."

"I *still* don't think handling criminals with kid gloves is appropriate, though. You can't be all easy on them, treating them like kids, and expect them not to do it again either, you know?"

"Of course not. We don't treat them like children – or 'go easy on them,' as you put it. But we don't abuse them, either. The global minimums for all local peoplements mandate that criminals – or offenders of the commonweal – must be educated further than they have been educated. That noble pursuit – education – *often* remedies the majority of problems that lead to crime. Some require a great deal more education to cut through the layers of trauma and abuse that covers up and clouds their authentic selves. We, as a society, in order to treat all fairly and give each person every benefit, presume that the each individual is basically good and that basic goodness needs to be discovered through Socratic inquiry. That is why the first and most useful rehabilitation method is education. In order for an offender to be 'corrected,' the individual must understand and agree that what they did was wrong. Do you understand?"

"Of course."

"Good. That's where we start when we educate them. And we go from there – morality classes, history classes, empathy classes, and so on. Understanding is cultivated through the most potent power a commonweal has... education."

"Education," I scoffed sarcastically. "*That's* how you deal with criminals here? Put them behind a desk and give them books?"

"That's precisely how. As I said before, Amoenians generally believe in the goodness that resides deep in the heart of humankind. Think of our rehabilitation centers, that is, what you call prisons – as schools for the morally corrupted. It is in these schools that morally corrupted individuals are taught what rudimentary school failed to teach them – kindness, care, and concern for others – in other words, the most sacred and important elements that humanity must cultivate to form true commonweals.

"Those who break the covenant of the commonwealth – the offenders – generally fall into two major categories: material and carnal offenses. Material offenses include all manner of stealing and vandalism... any breach against a brother, sister, or the commonweal's property. Carnal offenses, on the other hand, include all violent crimes and assaults: any breach against another's body."

"But, Sophia," I interjected, "earlier, you said that human beings are formed early in life insofar as morality is concerned. Wouldn't that, by *your own* admission, make these individuals – these criminals or offenders or whatever you want to call them – wouldn't that make them lost causes?"

Sophia bent over and scooped another shiny stone off the trail before answering. As she inspected it, my eyes wandered to the backyard of the house we were passing. There I watched a man using something that looked like a lawnmower – only smaller – to cut grass. I knew it was a lawnmower because I could smell the freshly cut grass all around me and because my eyes began to water with allergies. I realized that machines like lawnmowers, then, were acceptable in this society. I reasoned they didn't take jobs away and that the lawnmower itself was probably made by hand. As I made that observation, Sophia replied:

"Amoenians do not generally believe in such a thing as a lost cause. If we generally take the position that humankind is good, then, for the most part, the actions of humans must be intended to be generally good – either for themselves or others. If most human intentions are generally good, then evil is often a misdirected good. This misdirected good is usually good directed toward oneself and not toward others. In other words, evil is usually borne of selfishness. We generally view evil as a wish to fulfill one's own desire at the expense of another's material goods or carnal well-being. Evil, following this logic, is often the result of a lack of understanding or a lack of empathy on the part of the offender. In Amoena Vieta, we *teach*, not imprison or punish. There is no such thing, then, as a human being who is beyond help. There are only different levels of need. Some need much more education or learning than others."

I nodded. We were past the noise of the lawnmower now, and I could hear the trickling water of the running stream nearby.

"All offenders," Sophia continued, "are placed into one of three educational programs: Material education is composed to eradicate the first class of crimes. Carnal education is the second. Conjunction education mixes the two. Conjunction education is for those offenders who commit both carnal and material crimes."

"But, Sophia," I objected as I raised my voice in disbelief, "that is no deterrent at all! It's like simply saying, 'Go to school' to anyone who does anything wrong. School won't deter them from doing it again. That's only intellectual knowledge. It's not emotional knowledge... the knowledge that if you commit a crime, there will be pain inflicted upon you. *That's* a deterrent."

Sophia stopped instantly in the gravel and turned to face me. "How can you say that without having seen or known the composition of a detention center? Do you think spending time in a detention education center is pleasant? They are different from the education centers every peoplement has. Were you ever in the war machine of your country... the military?"

"No," I said, "but my Dad was. He was in my country's marine corps. He talked about it constantly and always had friends over who served with him. They all talked about it."

"If you have heard about what their training was like, then you probably have a concept of what our rehabilitation centers are like. Think of our detention center education as a type of boot camp of learning. One cannot come and go, leaving whenever they please, as can one in our education centers. Our rehabilitation centers are forced education, administered by the closest thing Amoenians have to what you call the police. Well-educated citizens serve the commonweal by teaching the morally corrupted in our rehabilitation centers. They cannot use physical violence. They cannot use force to teach. But they are trained in peaceful coercion and other nonviolent means by which they can get through to morally corrupted individuals. Make no mistake, John, offenders of the commonweal are treated humanely at *all* times. Rehabilitation centers are not places for endless punishment but rather for rehabilitation and learning. But be aware, it is by no means a desirable place to reside. The offenders are removed from a society wherein they are clothed, fed, and kindly treated. They are taken away from a society in which they enjoyed more freedoms and human dignity than any other society under the sun in the history of humanity. And in lieu of the pleasure of that society, offenders are submitted to grueling education both night and day. It is both a humane *and* effective criminal justice system that aims at moral rehabilitation. And that, we decided, should be the goal of a criminal justice system within the walls of a true commonweal."

"How long does this grueling education last?"

"Until the offender demonstrates that she or he can understand and abide by the core principle of our commonweal: concern for others."

"Who determines this demonstration of change? Who is given this god-like authority to decide who has been educated well enough and who has not?"

"The same system that has watched over other positions of authority from the very start: a system of checks and balances. No one person is given god-like authority in our system. Power is always spread out over our society as clouds are spread across the sky. Specific public judges and an elected panel of psychologists must review the offender and assess her or his progress. At least two-thirds of the officials – the judge and the panel of psychologists appointed to the offender's case – have to agree that the offender is no longer a material or carnal threat to the commonweal. It is only after that kind of assessment that the offender is granted freedom again.

"Similarly, an elected *commission on crime* group overviews the rehabilitation centers in every peoplement. They are obligated to monitor constantly that none of the offender's eternal rights are violated. Because as I noted, even offenders must always retain their eternal rights. Otherwise, the commonweal would fail to protect one of the most marginalized and disadvantaged groups, the morally corrupt.

"The peoplement is given the power to appoint the head of the detention center, and the head of the detention center is obligated to oversee the teachers at the detention center. The people monitor the commission of crime groups they elect under the eyes of the media. So, you see, John, the power, like always, lies within the people's broad arms. A true commonwealth cannot function otherwise."

"I see," I said as we walked along a part of the path that the stream ran along. I bent over, reached down, put my hand into the cool, refreshing water of the stream, and closed my eyes in delight. I was pleased by how cool the water felt on my hand. I cupped my hand, lifted out a small amount of water and washed my face with it. The cool, cleansing sensation of the water on my face felt simply wonderful. After the refreshment, I turned my head toward Sophia and asked, "So that's it, though? Grueling education and nothing more?"

"It seems that you have been conditioned to actually *want* some sort of state-imposed brutality to be committed against offenders of the commonweal, John. But as I said before, you will not find that in Amoena Vieta.

"Perhaps you'll be happy to know that it is not only education in a classroom. The offenders must spend a part of every day in the rehabilitation center doing manual labor. This is part of their education.

Most offenders are required to perform service for the commonwealth so that they may learn to work for the common good. They build roads and bridges under close supervision. They run animal shelters and help others in need of assistance in our commonwealth. Let me be clear, though… no offender would get a job for the commonweal if someone else was unemployed. But, if there is full employment, which there almost always is, the offender would be put to work making global and local minimums: always under close supervision, of course. But, as I said, all labor our offenders undertake is educational. It is all for the commonwealth. And our ability to reform offenders using work for the commonwealth and textbook education is exponential. Some offenders take years, while others take weeks or even days. Still, others must be educated for most of their lives, using every appeal to reason our educational system has. But there are a few instances where the individual does not change for the better."

"Okay," I said as the seed of this new, kinder, more compassionate mode of viewing and eliminating crime was planted in my mind, "There is one thing that you have not made better, though."

"What's that John?" Sophia asked genuinely.

"Well, you say that the power in Amoena Vieta always lies with the people by virtue of a much more empowering democracy. Yet, you also say that the people must be educated in order to understand how to wield their democratic power. And you certainly have composed a wonderful system of education to ensure that the people are well educated. But it seems to me that the education they get is theoretical. It is on morality, critical thinking, literature, empathy... all the subjects we saw and that you talked about so far. What I'm getting at is their education – or at least what you've shown me – does not teach people about the current events occurring within society. The knowledge of what is going on in the common-weal, and especially what those elected are doing, is almost as essential as the critical thinking skills they learn in rudimentary school. In order for people to be these 'philosopher kings,' they must have constant knowledge of current events."

"Let me use a concrete example to explain what I'm trying to say," I told her as I realized an allusion to Plato just came out of my mouth, "How can the citizens analyze the job of the commission on crime they elected unless they are constantly educated on precisely what the commission on crime is doing?"

Sophia laughed softly and glanced at the warm sun still shining on us, although it was markedly lower in the sky. "That is a fine question," she said, and my body brewed with intellectual pride. "First of all," she continued, "The people can stay informed – feel connected – on the goings on in the commonweal without much personal effort due to the small size of the local peoplement. This aspect of Amoenian culture and politics – the limited population size – makes knowing what is going on in one's peoplement, and therefore, makes one's democratic duty to the peoplement, far, far easier than one filled with a great number of individuals. When each person knows every other person in the peoplement, it is not hard for people to be connected to one another and for the discourse of the goings on in the to be easily known to everyone. Put simply, smaller populations make well-informed populations, and well-informed populations make democracy flourish.

"The second component that educates individuals on current events and fuels Amoenian democracy is what I am about to show you," she said before raising her left arm and pointing ahead to a long, wide blue building a short distance up the path. "It is essential to every peoplement and is essential to all of Amoena Vieta. Come on and I will show you our media," she said, and we walked side by side toward the blue building that drew closer with every step.

CHAPTER 7

MEDIA

We went up the gravel path to a white door in the center of the wide, blue building. It reminded me of the water purification building, except there were no lasers before the entrance and it was not secluded. The metal door in the middle had writing on it in Amoenish. I could not make any sense of it, so I broke the silence by asking Sophia what it read.

"It is the declaration that every member of the media makes. Every peoplement has a variation of the global media's pledge of honesty and full disclosure. The pledge recognizes that the media has an inherent and immense obligation to present honest, fully disclosed information to the members of society. The pledge states that the media must be the eyes of the public and has a sacred duty to inform," she said, and as she spoke, I followed her eyes as they read the words on the door. As she finished, she turned, looked at me, and said, "That's not everything – but it's the basic message of the pledge."

I stepped back from the door and took a long look at the wide, blue building that was sprawled out before me. On its top stood a marble statue of what looked like a gigantic bird.

"What is that, Sophia?" I said and pointed to the figure atop the building.

"It's an owl, John. That is the symbol of the media… in regions that have owls, that is."

"Why?' I asked, confused just as to why the symbol of the media would be an owl.

"Because the media is supposed to go after news on behalf of the commonweal, much like an owl goes after its prey. Media is obligated to stop at nothing and be able to report the news wherever it lay," she said as she looked at me and pointed to her eyes with her middle and index finger as if to say the media and owl share great vision. "Now, let's go in," she continued without waiting for my response. Sophia immediately put her hand over a small mechanism, and the door opened immediately and almost noiselessly. We walked inside.

* * *

The smell of ink and toner flooded my nose the moment I entered the door. I stood at the bottom of what appeared to be a giant circle and glanced around the room at a panorama of glass. Behind the glass rooms were people and electronics. Television screens, computers, computer monitors, and printers filled the area behind the glass. And even though the glass was there, I could hear the constant sound

of muffled voices as the Amoenians discussed something... what, I didn't know.

Sophia and I were not alone in the circular vestibule in which we stood. Once I took in
the general scene that resided behind the glass, I
looked around the room in which we stood where
there were ten to fifteen people. Each was sitting
on one of the benches in the vestibule, and as my
eyes swept over them, I noticed that each one of
them was looking intently at different individuals
behind the glass. I listened closely as they spoke
to each other, and the whole time they spoke, not
even one of them ever took their eyes off the people talking and working and typing behind the
glass in front of us.

"What's going on here, Sophia?" I finally asked.
As usual, Sophia did not speak until I asked her a
question. She always just let me take it all in.

"What you are watching," Sophia said, "is the
unending quest of the media to discover and disclose
the goings-on throughout the commonweal. This is
the media hub in this peoplement of Amoena Vieta.
Each has one similar to it."

I smiled and quietly counted the people behind
the glass. All in all, there were about twenty people.

"Only twenty people uncover the news?"

"Yes, John – excluding most of the reporters,
of course. There are the others," she lifted her right

hand to her chin and looked ahead at the people in behind the glass, "There are a number of reporters who are out on assignment."

I looked at her with surprise. "But don't there need to be more reporters – more media employees – to uncover all the news?"

"No, what you see is sufficient. The media in Amoena Vieta is not charged with uncovering *all* the news in the commonwealth. That would be an impossible task for that amount of people," she said before she stepped forward toward the glass and breathed on it, making it foggy with condensation. She took her sleeve and wiped off a small smudge on the glass before she continued, "The individuals behind the glass – the local media – have but three jobs. Those jobs are to uncover and disclose all they can about the goings on in the local peoplement, to watch over and disclose information about the peoplement's treatment centers and oversight commissions, and, to ethically report the information to those who the peoplement and treatment centers serve: in other words, to tell the people what's going on."

"That's it?"

"That's all that's necessary." she replied promptly.

"So, then, the only job of the media is to accurately and ethically present local politics and the goings on at treatment centers: and nothing more?

No human-interest stories, no crossword puzzles, no sports, no funnies, no lifestyle section in the local newspaper?"

"No, none of those things are included. Those items are not necessary knowledge for the well-functioning of a commonweal. They are entertainment. And as entertainment, they have their place in the private sector of the Amoenian economy. They all exist in most peoplements but they are purchased in magazine form at local stores for profit. Local and global media are provided to the public for free as an Eternal Right. It falls under the right to accessible information and knowledge of all public information and the right to a *free* and open press. The essential information that media centers in peoplements produce is part of the global minimums. Therefore, everyone is, by right, consistently informed about their government.

"That's why every single day, Amoenians receive two media sections that are delivered promptly to their computer. One is from their local people's media center, and the other is from the global servicement's media center."

A tall, blonde man got up from the bench behind us and, to my surprise, sprinted to the glass and pounded on it with hard, powerful slams as if his arms were a hammer and the glass was a nail. I watched as a dark-haired woman in a blue shirt walked calmly over to him from the other side of the glass. She made a few hand gestures that, after a minute or two, seemed to calm the man slightly. Once he was a little calmer, she pulled a lever and a small piece of glass slid aside and made a small portal to the other side of the glass. The man immediately entered the room, and the woman promptly closed the opening.

I watched the blonde man and dark-haired woman speak to one another, and in no time, the man was gesturing wildly with his hands again.

"What does the global media report?" I asked Sophia as my attention returned to our conversation. The room fell back to the murmurs of voices after the man's violent, loud interruption.

"The global media reports on the activities of the *global* servicement."

"And nothing more?"

"Nothing more," she said, "Again, the private sector produces all entertainment – not the public media."

"Wait a minute!" I objected vehemently. "You mean to tell me that the media is a *public* entity in Amoena Vieta? How can it be honest and fair if it is part of the peoplement. Isn't it then biased and influenced by the interests of the peoplement?"

She took a deep breath and responded, "The media *is* public, John, and so you are correct to say that. But I think you are mistaking what is meant by the public here. Public goods are goods that the commonweal has decided to belong to everyone. The news about what the elected officials in the global and local peoplements is, by definition, then, a public good. But the media – local *or* global – has absolutely no dependence on a formal affiliation with the local peoplement or global servicement. In fact, one of the oversight groups which are created are global and local media oversight commissions. These commissions are the individuals responsible for watching over the reporters, editors, and print-ers you see here," she said and pointed toward the glass. "Do you see that woman talking to the man who was just let through the other side of the glass?" she motioned toward the woman with dark hair and blue shirt.

"Yes," I said immediately.

"She is the head of the media in this peoplement. She hires, fires, and oversees the publishing of local news here. And she is elected. Not appointed. She is elected *by the people* of the peoplement. Therefore, she can be removed by a majority vote at any time during her tenure here. That is why the media is publicly owned in Amoena Vieta."

I listened and just as Sophia finished speaking, the irate man who went behind the glass slowed his wild gesturing and calmed down. A few moments later – or what seemed like a few moments – he shook the woman's hand and came back to the other side of the glass where Sophia and I stood.

"What was that about?" I asked, "Why was that man so angry? Who is he?"

"He," Sophia said, and with her right arm, she swept the air in such a way as to gesture to all the people around us, "is one of these people. He is a citizen of the local peoplement. As such, he is exercising his right to oversee the local media. The man was probably arguing with the head of the media over the details of a story. Many of the citizens do the same. They serve as another check and balance on the ever-important presses throughout Amoena Vieta. The residents of each local peoplement are free to help their media stay fair in their subjective assessments of the occurrences they report on."

"So in every peoplement there is a local media like this one? And in every peoplement, are there citizens who watch over it... in addition to the media commission?"

"Yes," she replied, and I watched a short, stocky woman walk through the door that opened in the glass in front of us. She began speaking to the woman in the same irate way the man before her spoke. As Sophia and I watched her, I felt something like a fan come on, and a soft, cool wind blew across our faces from that point on while we were in the media center. It wasn't a minute too soon, either – it was getting a little stuffy in the room.

"And," Sophia continued, "there is also global media. The global media has specific jurisdiction over global political stories, just as the local media have a specific jurisdiction over local political stories.

"There are, of course, also other global media that cover the rest of the news and events of interest to the citizens of Amoena Vieta. But those news and events are not fundamental to the commonweal."

"So, it's mainly political stuff that's covered in the global media and local medias... and any other story that affects the whole commonweal. I got it."

"You see, John, the only way a true democratic commonwealth can survive is through an informed population. That is why global and local media in Amoena Vieta have elected officials running them and yet remain unregulated by any form of legislation from the government. We agree that the media must always remain outside of the grasp of elected officials because that helps to ensure their honesty, which translates into a more informed public. A well-informed public is essential for democracy to thrive.

"The local and global media – are obligated to deliver the political news of the commonwealth to the computer of every Amoenian in their jurisdiction. If they do not fulfill this obligation at any time, the elected watchdog of the media can be removed by popular vote and a new media oversight representative will be elected who will hire a staff of her or his choosing.

"The citizens are not obligated to read their papers, of course. But we have found that it is rare for an individual to not read their global or local papers."

As I listened to her speak, I felt the air from the fan and paused a few moments to enjoy it before replying, "If the public is not obligated to read the paper, why do so many people do it?"

"Because in each local peoplement of 700 households, everyone knows everyone else. Either they know each other as a friend or as an acquaintance – it can be no other way in a place with that limited number. In a place where everyone knows everyone else, the vice of vanity is automatically cultivated and reared in the human psyche. Therefore, the need for a good reputation becomes essential to most individuals in each local peoplement. To be seen in a good light is paramount to most people because it fosters something everyone desires – a good self-concept. Since people often succumb to seeing themselves the way they are viewed by others, the community around them can deeply affect the way they see themselves and therefore affect their behavior. Almost no one desires to be out of the social loop of society or the common discourse. If they do, then they are free, as the philosopher Sartre advocated, to express their individuality in any way they wish. However, we find *the vast* majority of people, in adolescence and adulthood, strive to keep a good reputation with the society. Therefore, they stay up on the news. This and the fact that voting is mandatory are the two factors that ensure an informed and engaged electorate. These two factors are the lifeblood of our democracy."

"I guess you're right, Sophia – those two factors are ways of ensuring a well-functioning democracy." I chuckled as I went on, "Unless, of course, the people don't understand the news. I mean, I've read stories in my newspapers wherein I couldn't extract the main point after reading it several times."

Sophia smiled as if she somehow anticipated the statement. "In the Amoenian way of striving for simplicity, we have made our global and local media as understandable as possible." As she spoke, I watched a little bronze woman go in and shake the media woman's hand the same way the man did before returning to the section of the room in which we stood. The little woman even had the same kind of pleased grin on her face as the man who preceded her.

"Even with a highly educated populace," Sophia continued, "there is still a possibility for the horrors of sloth to possess the hearts of the people in a society, due to genetic or environmental factors. So, for our lethargic citizens, as well as for our less-than-average-intelligence citizens and our citizens who haven't a long attention span, we have made adjustments. The global and local media compose their papers in such a way as to keep all people informed.

"Each political story is headlined just as I'm sure they are in the papers you are used to reading, John. But after the headline, the story does not immediately begin."

"What does begin?"

"To make the article more accessible, our papers outline the story in such a way that it is easily and quickly understandable and accessible. Then, after the outline, the story begins."

I looked at Sophia confusedly at what I thought was an incredibly strange way to organize news stories. She put her right palm out toward me and pumped it twice in my direction in an obvious attempt to tell me to hear it out.

"The outline," she continued, "does just that – outlines the article by providing the thesis and main points supporting it. For instance, let's take one of last week's major stories," she said as she walked to the back of the room, next to the bench. There, a computer rested on a small desk with a seat in front of it. It took Sophia a few moments of touching the screen and type before she brought up what I assumed was the local peoplement's newspaper on the screen. After a moment or two of reading it, she continued, "The local representative of the peoplement put forth legislation suggesting a raise on the *commonwealth commission*, which is the term Amoenians use for taxes, in an attempt to raise the global minimum of apples in our peoplement to two bags per week. In order to produce the extra apples in this peoplement, an apple farm would have to be set up. The place the representatives of this local peoplement are interested in using for the apple farm is the land where there is an old public playground," she said. I walked over so I could be next to her to see the screen. As she spoke, I watched her eyes go from left to right on the screen, "It seems the representatives passed this law, but the peoplement promptly vetoed it. Therefore, it was not made into law. The story appeared in the paper this way," she said before grabbing a piece of yellow scrap paper off the desk on which the computer rested. She pulled what looked like a pen out of her pocket and wrote,

"Article Headline: Commonwealth Rejects Extra Apple Local Minimum and Keeps Playground Instead

Article Outline:

I.   Peoplement representatives push bill to get rid of playground in an attempt to have higher local minimum of apples.

II.   Commonwealth swiftly votes down proposal by slim 52% margin."

After she scribbled this on the scrap paper, she looked at me and spoke, "That's how the headline and outline of the article appear. Then the story begins, weaving those points into a narrative. The article is where all the details are given. But the essence, if well done, gives the citizens all they need to know."

I nodded as the logic of the paper's layout slowly become sensible and attractive to me. While Sophia spoke, I watched individuals come and go from the media building entrance and was delighted to see a steady flow of new faces entering all the time.

But as I thought over what Sophia had said, one notion stuck in my mind. I decided I had to ask about it. But I asked with hesitancy because I knew it was a question that had divided many nations and philosophies of government from the dawn of civilization to the present day, meaning, all of recorded history. But I was certain that it would never stop being an issue – even in her day. So, I asked,

"What exactly did you mean when you said taxes – or, as you just put it, commonwealth commission?"

Sophia's face brightened instantly, and I heard a different kind of laugh – a bolder, more guttural laugh from deep within her chest rather than the soft, giggly laughter that I was accustomed to. After she recovered from her laughing spell, her face broke into a smile, and she said, "I was wondering when you'd get around to asking that. Our commonwealth commission – or tax – system is simple. And it is the last part of Amoena Vieta that I want to show you. Come on." She beckoned with her hand as she began moving toward the door. I hurried behind her, and we left the soothing cool air of the media center and walked out into the warm, consistent and comforting light of the sun outside.

CHAPTER 8

COMMONWEALTH COMMISSION (TAXES)

The sun was descending in the Amoenian sky by the time we left the media building. It was just as bright and luminous as it was all day, only now it was lower in the sky, something like the way the evening sun appears on a lazy summer day. As we strolled down the path, I heard the noise of the stream and the songs of birds I'd never heard before. By this time, I could hear the occasional croaking of what reminded me of the bullfrogs at my grandpa's summer house when I was a little boy. But the sounds weren't the sounds of bullfrogs – the sounds were deeper and richer, throatier if you can believe it. They were *like* bullfrog sounds. Once it got a little later, the threatening, soft cadence of katydids entered my ears. Only the orchestra of repetitious songs they played was louder and more synchronized than the katydids I was used to hearing.

Before long, I was able to push the melodies of the Amoenian night into the background of my mind so that I could consider all that I had seen and could remember.

I thought about the emphasis on simplicity and democracy that ran like a carpet under all – or almost all – the societal systems of Amoena Vieta. And I thought about the concept of global minimums and local minimums, too. I was and am very attracted to these ideals because they are so compassionate and humanistic. But it seemed that to put these ideals in place, bigger government, or 'servicement' as Sophia called it, was necessary. Even if the government was kept in check by more checks and balances than I could imagine – the bottom line is that it was still more government. Before long, I could hear Dad's voice in my mind, complaining that the only good government is no government.

"Global minimums?" Dad's voice resonated in my mind as Sophia, and I walked side by side, "What are they actually saying? I'll tell you. Big government. It's Uncle Sam. It's taxes galore. Communism, that's what it is. I'll tell you what they can do with their global minimums..."

Dad's objection seemed valid – even if he never did phrase it very eloquently. And I'd heard lots of people voice the same objection. So, I decided to ask Sophia. Of course, I left out Dad's coarseness.

"You know" I said, "I'm thinking about the whole setup Amoena Vieta has, and there's one thing that bothers me."

"What's that?"

"Well, between all the servicement positions that Amoenian peoplement – both global and local

– has, along with the global and local minimums provided for all Amoenians, the taxes here must be phenomenally high. I bet Amoenians have a tax system that is just overwhelmingly complex."

Sophia shook her head. "It's just the opposite of what you propose. Amoenian servicement does collect a tax. We call it a 'commission' because it is a fee for services rendered by the servicement. Our version of taxes is far simpler than any industrialized nation ever composed. And it is true that this commission or tax is high in Amoena Vieta. But *services* are just as high as the taxes. After all, the entire goal of taxes should be to attain services that benefit the commonwealth. Everyone in the community pays a fee out of what material wealth they have. That pot of material wealth then provides services for everyone. That's why we call the commonwealth a common-wealth. Taxes are the material price of living in a community. At the same time, taxes create the benefits one derives from living with others and does so in the form of services. So why could any citizen begrudge taxation if they know that it is accounted for and going to the common good?"

I laughed at her naivety, "Because, Sophia, we never know if it is actually going to the *common good,* do we?"

"In Amoena Vieta, everyone is ensured that the commonwealth commission is appropriated for the common good. All of the commonwealth commission – every single bit of exchange that is paid to the peoplement – is, by global law, accounted for in the local peoplement and global servicement media. Every day there is a section in the global and local media in which it is published. And every piece of unitrade paid in taxes is detailed throughout the year. On top of this, all citizens are *always* permitted to look deeper into the records of how the commonwealth commission was spent. The elected commonwealth commission board – an oversight group autonomous of both the global and local peoplements – get together to review the figures each day to ensure they are accurate. And the citizens always have access to all the records."

As Sophia spoke, the transport rolled by, ever so softly tickling the ears with the faint hum of its engine. I watched and listened as it passed before formulating my next question.

"Okay. So Amoena Vieta has ensured the accountability of its peoplement and servicement. Amoena Vieta also ensures services for all the taxes it receives. But I bet the taxes are suffocating in Amoena Vieta. How can't they be if all those services are provided out of the commonwealth commission?"

"John, the services created out of that fund are provided for the benefit of all. No service provided by the government is *not* for the common good. And so, a higher rate of commonwealth commission should not bother anyone in the least. A higher commonwealth commission just means a higher rate of services."

"But that's not true," I objected. "The treatment centers we keep passing for drug and alcohol abuse and dependence, mental illness, and a slew of other ailments – those treatment centers are coming from taxpayers. Yet, they are not for the benefit of the whole population. But the whole of the population is paying for them, right?"

"Yes. Commonwealth commissions are the funding for the treatment centers."

"Well, then, how can you say that services are provided for all?"

Sophia picked up, examined, and skipped a stone along the gravel trail before responding, "If we as a society do not aid the person suffering from alcoholism or drug addiction by showing him how to train his body not to need alcohol or drugs, and if we as a society do not use our material, empathetic, and psychological means to help those with mental disorders to escape their mental torments, what do you think happens to that society, John? What do you think happens.... besides the moral decay that can't help but accompany a lack of concern for others in society?"

"What happens to *society*? Nothing. To the individuals? They suffer," I replied.

"And you do agree that society has an obligation to try to minimize the suffering of its members, right, John?"

"Yes. But that was not my question," I said defiantly as I watched a brightly colored insect flutter by, "I know that it is the kinder and more compassionate thing for society to do. But the fact remains that treatment centers do *not* provide services to all of the population. Instead, they funnel taxpayer – or commonwealth commission – unitrade to a small segment of the population. Therefore, the commonwealth commission is not always providing a service for the whole population. In this case, they are providing services only to a very small segment."

"But that is not true," Sophia replied instantly and assertively. "When society allows the sick or the ailing to suffer, there is not just a *moral* cost to society. There is a *tangible, visible cost*, too. The disease of the drug addicted will likely compel him to do things that he would not otherwise to do attain the substance for which his body lusts. The agony of the person struggling with mental illness may cause them to lash out at loved ones or others. In short, the ailments of the individual, when untreated, quite often lead to the ailments of others in society. We are all interconnected by our humanity *and* our proximity to one another. What affects one, then, often can't help but affect others. In this way, the commonwealth commission used for treatment centers benefits the whole of society. It helps society to take care of these individuals... both morally *and* practically.

"Furthermore, John, taking care of them is more fiscally advantageous. Where do the sick, those struggling physically, the downtrodden, the addicted often end up?"

"In pris-, I mean, in rehabilitation centers," I said reflexively.

"Exactly. And incarceration costs unitrade. Therefore, either way you look at it, society is responsible for financially aiding these citizens. The question becomes whether financial aid should be used to pick up these fallen citizens, most of whom tripped by fate, genes, or circumstance, or by putting bars in front of them? The cost is a variable that remains about the same. It is a matter of *how* we want to spend the wealth. We could spend it preventatively by treating people and offering them services. Or, we can spend it on incarceration if they find they way into the legal system."

"Right. I see that logic."

"Don't you agree, then, that it is more compassionate and more pragmatic for society to pick up the least fortunate through the use of the commonwealth commission and treatment centers? Don't you agree that it ends up costing the taxpayer – the society – less in both morality and material goods in the long run in most cases?"

"Yes, I think I can see what you are saying."

"Good. But let me clarify further. The difference between commonwealth commissions going toward treatment centers and water purification plants are as follows. Water purification plants provide a service that *directly* helps the entire society by directly providing water to all. Treatment centers are providing a service for the entire society indirectly by helping specific individuals. The bottom line is this... both water purification plants *and* treatment centers are helping society: one directly and the other indirectly. Do you agree?"

"Yes," I said before feeling the stubble on my face as I thought. "But it seems to me that you could make that argument to justify any spending in society. For instance, you could justify that exorbitant salaries for global leaders paid by tax dollars are good and necessary for society because those salaries encourage the leader to do more work for that society. Do you see? All one needs is a good lawyer to twist your logic around!"

Sophia grinned, "If the voting public were not schooled in critical thinking, then yes, you would be right. Leaders who base their arguments on fallacious thought could rise to power in a democratic system and become detrimental to society. That is why no institution is more important than education, and no value is more important than compassionate understanding in Amoena Vieta. A good education, that is, good critical thinking skills reveal the self-interested greed and fallacious thought of any politician who made an argument such as the one you just posed. In most local peoplements, an argument such as the one you've made would be shot down on the basis of proof. There is no evidence to suggest that representatives do a better job of representing when they are paid well. This is evidenced by thousands of years wherein that was the case. Better pay has never produced better leaders. I hope you can now understand why the educational system in every local peoplement in Amoena Vieta is given such immense importance. Any democracy is dependent on two things... the goodness of humankind and education of everyone. One is innate and constantly cultivated by the world. The other must be given to the individual by the society.

"But of course, human variation and self-expression being as it is, there are always exceptions to every rule. It is up to most of the people in the local peoplement. It is always up to the majority of people, so long as they do not trample over the eternal rights of the minority. Those are the lines the majority can never cross."

I listened to the symphony of the insects playing their song in the night air as the evening drifted over Amoena Vieta.

"Okay. Taxes – or commonwealth commissions – are collected solely for services that affect all. I understand that. You have shown how things like treatment centers affect all of society. But you still have not told me *how* commonwealth commissions are collected. Is it a flat tax, a progressive tax, – or something entirely different?"

She took a deep breath and furrowed her brow before she began to speak, "As I noted before, Amoenians generally feel that, as Jesus said, much will be expected of those who have been given a great deal. This general philosophy guides our commonwealth commissions in most peoplements, and it is the philosophy utilized by our global servicement for almost the entirety of Amoena Vieta's existence. From those who have a great deal of the material goods in society, much is expected in commonwealth commission so that they may benefit the whole society."

My knowledge of the New Testament kicked in, and I argued, "But Sophia, I believe Jesus was referring to God in that passage. I believe Jesus was telling us what God expects from us, not what we should expect from each other."

"You are right, John. But the general principle of the statement rings true in most people's spirit.

We are not asserting that the people are a God-like entity. We *are* asserting that those who are blessed enough to have been given much in their existence have a moral debt to those who have *not* been given much. The fact that we are all put in this existence together and depend on one another for so much necessitates that we help one another. Each is asked by society to give according to their ability to give. And so those who have much must give much for the good of the common weal, and those who have little must give little – not as a whole amount, but as a percentage of their income."

I saw nothing but a windy road up ahead and rows of houses mingled with dense forest on either side.

"I understand what you are saying, Sophia. But it sounds like Amoena Vieta is drenched with heavy commonwealth commissions."

She laughed and shook her head, "Why should Amoenians begrudge heavy commissions if they *are* getting representation from their commission in the form of services? If they can *see* exactly how every bit of their unitrade was spent for the good of society, why should they mind the commonwealth commission?"

"Because it robs them of some of their economic freedom."

Sophia shot back, "In Amoena Vieta, self-expression is almost unlimited. But we recognize that *some* economic self-expression must be limited to provide a materially equitable, socially conscious, compassionate society wherein all have *enough*. I concede that some economic freedom must be sacrificed for the good of the commonweal. The question is about values. Amoenians value that everyone has enough more than they value unlimited material expression. We value it because we see it as right.

"And if this appeal to compassion and morality is not enough for some Amoenians, they need only to consider the fact that the higher rates of commonwealth commission simply translate into more services provided for all. The commission means there are no more worries about having enough food, water, health care, clothing, etc. *These* are the primary economic fruits that are reared from Amoenian commissions. Global and local minimums are provided to all."

"Do all peoplements use the progressive commonwealth commission you are describing? I mean, if there is such a range of viewpoints across Amoena Vieta, there should be lots of different ideas for how commonwealth commission should be collected, right?"

"No, all local peoplements do not adopt the progressive structure of their commonwealth commission. In fact, the only political commonalities that all peoplements share is that they all recognize the eternal rights of human beings and abide by global decrees that pass a majority vote. Some have progressive commonwealth commission systems and others have flat tax systems. That is entirely up to them," she said before turning toward me, looking me in the eyes, and responding seriously, "so long as their commonwealth commission system provides the basic necessities to all members of the commonwealth. Any system of commission that fails to do that cannot be used in Amoena Vieta."

I picked up a red stone on the path and skipped it across the nearby creek in a slow-moving spot. The rock skipped several times before splashing into the water and frightening a nearby duck. Then I continued, "The way you are describing it, it seems to me that local peoplements are the only entity that charges a commonwealth commission to the people. The global servicement doesn't collect taxes, then?"

She nodded. "No, it doesn't. You see, Amoenians believe the tax system, like all aspects of the servicement, must *never* become inaccessible to the people because it is for the benefit of the people. So, there is only *one* commonwealth commission. It is only collected by the local peoplement but overseen by the global servicement. And the vast majority of the peoplements – 99% – choose a progressive system to collect the commonwealth commission."

I stopped in shock on the gravel path. "*One* tax? That's it? My country has taxes from at least four different levels of govern – servicement. And there are so many taxes, too. Income tax, social security tax, medicare tax, state income tax, sales tax, property tax, payroll tax, transfer tax, capital gains tax," I said, recalling as many as I could, "and the list goes on and on!"

"We are familiar with the tax code of past nations. The tax codes of those nations were complex only so that government could muddy the waters of honest communication. They were made so complex as to silence any objection to their payment.

"Amoenians have never seen a *need* for more than one tax. The idea of taxing individuals more than once is both absurd and confusing. In fact, the double, triple, and quadruple taxation that you describe is beyond senseless. It was often used as a way to confuse the system and for servicement to cheat the people. Our Amoenian commonwealth commission is most often referred to as the *unitax*. This commission encompasses all the taxes you named. In addition, it is simple and understandable. Those two criteria... simplicity and comprehensibility, are what guide our system."

I was confused. "So, then, only one servicement collects the commonwealth commission– the local peoplement. That means that only the local peoplement provides services, right?"

"No. Only the local peoplement does collect the commonwealth commission. But *both* the global

servicement and local peoplement," she paused
thoughtfully, and I watched as her brow furrowed
and tightened the skin across her forehead, "*both*
share the one commission. All services are provided
for the people out of this one, simple commission."

"Then what income can be taxed?"

"All of it," Sophia replied reflexively. "The tax is
on all the material goods that one has accrued in that
cycle."

I was taken aback. "You make it sounds like there
aren't even any deductions,"

"What you call deductions, John, are not a part
of the Amoenian tax code."

I laughed. "So, then you're telling me that someone with, say, two children has to pay the same rate
as someone with one child? There are no deductions? That hardly seems fair or just."

"That's right, John, both would pay the same
rate. And many Amoenians, including myself, agree
with you – it's unfair. But I don't think you understand the logic of having no deductions...

"We have found that deductions primarily serve
only the craftiest and most dishonest members of
our society. However, it is true that deductions also
serve to help honest people. And general critical
thinking skills show us that we should not get rid
of the whole system if only part of the system is not
working.

"That's why we do not eliminate deductions on that basis alone," she said and as she spoke, the transport swiftly made its way past us, pushing the air into a soft breeze. "The other purpose of having no deductions is our way of encouraging population control. All too often, we have found the fact that dependent children count as deductions and serve as an incentive for some to bear children. In Amoena Vieta, there is only a finite amount of land and resources that we can utilize. And so, our people generally agree that *some* form of population control is necessary for the good of all."

I stood in shock. "So, you're telling me that Amoenians have economic sanctions in the tax code that discourage procreation?"

"The people have chosen this method as one form to deter rampant population growth. They have chosen other economic sanctions in addition to free birth control being available to all as other methods. The citizenry generally believes that this is the only way to preserve the freedom of individuals to procreate while, at the same time, deterring this procreation for the good of the whole."

"I guess it seems reasonable."

"The people of Amoena Vieta – religious and secular – seem to think so. It is, perhaps, the only humane way to administer a form of population control – that is, the use of economic sanctions.

Since there is virtually no war in Amoena Vieta, and since violent crime is dramatically reduced by Democratism, Amoenians *need* some form of population control to make it so that the production of goods and services does not lag behind the consumption of goods and services. Because if production ever does lag behind consumption, society will inevitably devolve back into the capitalist jungle so many industrialized nations of the world knew so well."

"I think I get the idea," I said before bending over to pick the most beautiful blue flower I'd ever laid my eyes on. "But you still haven't explained exactly how taxes are collected, Sophia. I mean, I understand the local peoplements are responsible for collecting them, and I understand that the global servicement takes a percentage of each local peoplement's taxes based on the number of services the global servicement is obligated to provide the people. You've said that Amoena Vieta's system is based on simplicity and accessibility. So, then, *how* does the local peoplement collect the commonwealth commission from the people?"

"I am glad you are truly beginning to understand the philosophical basis of Amoenian simplicity and goodwill toward every member of the human family, John," Sophia said with a proud smile on her face.

After a few moments, she continued, "Our local peoplments are mandated by the global servicement to engage in the direct withholding of wealth. This means that the local peoplement must take its percentage from your material goods *before* you even receive it. The peoplements are charged with this responsibility – the people are not.

"The residents of the local peoplement can figure out if they have taken the right amount of commission out because, as I said, there is only one tax, making the process remarkably simple. The amount that is taken from the citizen generally ranges anywhere from 20% to 80% of their unitrade, depending on the amount they have been blessed with and can afford to provide for the good of all. The local peoplement collects this amount all year round.

"And that's all there is to it. That's the entire simplified system as far as the citizens of Amoena Vieta are concerned."

I pulled the petals from the blue flower in my hand one by one. A buttery substance developed on my hand as I spoke,

"And the global servicement just takes its prescribed amount, according to a number of services the people have voted to have?"

"Yes. That's it," she smiled as if to congratulate me. "The global servicement takes what they need from the local peoplement in order to provide the services they are obligated to provide for the people – the global minimums."

"But what if a local peoplement shortchanges a person? What happens then?"

"Then that person can appeal to one of the checks and balances of the peoplement – in this case, they can appeal to the commonwealth commission group that they, the people, elected to oversee the local peoplment's collection of the commonwealth commission. The commission group then investigates the matter on behalf of the citizen and finds out whether the local peoplement has overcharged the citizen. And if the commission ever devolves into corruption or is ineffective, what do you think occurs then?"

I smiled. "They will be voted out of office and replaced."

"Now you're really getting it, John. Now you understand the power of the *people* in Amoena Vieta. The system is set up so it is always accessible to and adaptable for the masses.

"It is important to note that global law requires all peoplements to provide a paper trail for all taxes they collect. It is the job of the commonwealth commission group, the media, and ultimately, the people themselves to ensure that the local peoplement remains honest."

A little way down the path, I could see the reflection of the sun off of a large pond or a lake. I couldn't quite tell at first, but as we got closer, I saw that it was too big to be a pond – it was a very large, wide lake. It was in the oddest place... the path led right to it. There were houses, people, and a rabbit or a squirrel scattered here and there all along the path still, just as there had been throughout Amoena Vieta. The transport tracks still ran uninterrupted, too. But right smack in the middle of the path, there was the large body of water. Confusion descended upon me as to why Amoenians built the path right into this body of water. But I did not interrupt Sophia as she continued. She spoke fervently, and the tone of her voice was tinged with maternal seriousness, such that I think any man raised by a strong mother could recognize and should know never to interrupt.

"I have now taken you, John Matthews, on a cursory tour of Amoena Vieta. You have seen many things and I hope you don't forget them. Because I believe our society can help your society. Our society is grounded in and guided by the principle of love and has taken lessons from many of the mistakes of past societies. It is a society that is generally in a constant state of change because the minds of its inhabitants are constantly evolving, and, society can't help but reflect the minds that mold it. Amoena Vieta also acknowledges certain Eternal Rights that are fairly static. It is a society that recognizes that all people have certain rights, which form the only constant, almost unchangeable aspects of the covenant formed in Amoena Vieta. It is a society that has carried the torch of humanistic progress to new heights, as evidenced by its more compassionate, democratic structure than that of its predecessors.

"Do not forget that humankind can never rest in its attempt to improve its love for one another, which is achieved, in part, by improving the structure of the systems that compose its society. Do not allow erroneous doubt to infect your thoughts, lowering the bar that humanity strives to reach and telling you that society cannot always be made more perfect. And do not ever," her green eyes looked at me intensely as if she were looking into me, "do not ever doubt the light of goodness that shines brightly in the human soul and makes *love* our greatest and most powerful tool. Don't forget that God or nature or whatever you choose to call that greater force, has placed in your consciousness a little piece of everlasting guidance that you must cultivate and understand to the best of your ability. In other words, John, do not ever forget that to thine own self, you must be true."

As Sophia finished, we reached the lake. The water moved gently back and forth, splashing against the shore's irregularly shaped green and black rocks.

The sound was calming in a way that I have never experienced. It was as if it were pressing on a pressure point in my mind.

I nodded toward Sophia in awe of both her and the society she showed me. She smiled that big, bright, beautiful smile, and I felt her hand gently guiding me toward the water. I can't explain why, but it just seemed right to go into the water. I waded into it and was even more sedated by its warmth and welcoming nature. I automatically walked out toward the middle of the lake very slowly, and Sophia followed. When I reached a point where the water level was up to my chest, I stopped. I did not speak, and neither did Sophia. After several moments I felt her soft touch on my head. She gently applied pressure that I could have resisted if I wanted. But I didn't want to resist. I trusted her and felt only love toward her. I slowly descended into the warm water until it filled my nose and covered my head. I could have jumped up at any time and gotten out of the water, but I had no wish to do so. I somehow knew I had to be submerged.

EPILOGUE

He heard the rhythmic beeping of a machine nearby, along with the whirring of a machine next to him. He felt a large plastic structure stuck in his mouth and saw tubes emanating from it. His eyes followed the tubes to the machines that were at the side of his bed. He could see many tubes coming out of him. He lifted his hand up and felt a plastic tube in his nose that was not removable to the tug. It went far back into his nose and down his throat before emptying into his stomach. His hand moved over to his chest, where he felt wires that were connected directly to his skin via small, sticky patches. He traced these wires and saw that they went into a screen on the wall above his head. He saw needles in his arm connected to an IV which was on the other side of his bed. He had a metallic taste in his mouth that sickened him. John wanted water and tried to move but due to the apparatus he was confined to his current position.

There were more wires and other machinery. However, John did not occupy himself with them. Instead, he became consumed with fear and panic. He did not know where he was or why he was there. John looked like a protagonist from a Kafka novel and was filled with existential dread. He searched his mind for some rationale, logic, or reason for why this was and what had happened.

He continued to survey the room and saw that it was daytime. All shades were drawn, and it was overwhelmingly dark. However, he could see the beams of light trying to break through the shades in every direction. His nose was filled with the smell of death and disinfectant that seemed to pervade the room that he was in.

John waited a long time like this. He sat in terror and postulated what may have happened. After a long while, a slender Hispanic nurse with dark and wavy hair down to her shoulders walked into the room.

"Mr. Matthews! You're awake!" She said as she noticed his eyes were open and looking in all directions.

John could not talk. He lay there and tilted his head toward her with fearful brown eyes.

The young nurse came closer and asked him to perform a test. She put out her hands and asked him to squeeze them. She squeezed his toes and asked if he could feel it.

"You have been in a coma for a few days," the nurse said. "You have been in a very significant accident. We did not know if you would come out of it at all, never mind come out of it in just a few days," she said as she fixed his bed and pillows behind him.

"I'm going to get the doctor to let him know that you've awakened."

John nodded in response, and she could see that he was cognitively present. She walked over to the opposite side of the room from where John's bed was took out a pad and pen and made some notes. Then she left the room and John was alone again in his fear and uncertainty.

John noticed how much his body hurt. He noticed that he could not move his legs and that while one arm, his right arm, was able to move freely, the other one was not. He felt claustrophobic and the more he lay in the bed, the more he felt as if he had traversed from a dream directly into a nightmare.

Several minutes later, a tall, black man walked into the room. Like the nurse, he had a mask on and John could see his dark and serious eyes. He walked up to the bed and held the clipboard.

"Mr. Matthews, do you know where you are?"

John shook his head as best hc could amidst the pain and the encumbrances all around him.

"My name is Dr. Jones. I am a doctor at Scranton Hospital. You were brought here five days ago after a severe car accident. Do you understand what I'm saying to you right now?"

John nodded immediately.

"Good. Do you remember what happened?"

John looked alarmed. He took a few moments to try to recall what happened. He had vague premonitions but the memories were not accessible to him now. He shook his head at the doctor.

"You sustained some broken bones and contusions due to the accident. However you also hit your head very hard when your car tumbled over. You have sustained a brain injury. This is why you have all the equipment you have connected to you. We are monitoring your body's activities and will remove these machines once we are convinced your body can do them on its own. Please don't be alarmed, Mr. Matthews. This is standard procedure. We will know more as we gradually reduce your dependence on these machines and track your progress."

John nodded. As he nodded, there was anxiety that showed in his eyes.

"This is Maria, and she is one of your nurses. Do you see that wire with the white handle and the red button in the middle of the cone?" Dr. Jones asked in a deep and commanding voice.

John nodded. "That is the button that you can press anytime for Maria or one of the other nurses or staff to come to this room. I understand that you're in a very compromised position mentally, emotionally, and physically right now. I want you to know they are here if you have any concerns or if you need assistance. Please hang in there."

John was trying to move his lips to say something but could not say anything due to the tubes that were down in his throat.

"Please, Mr. Matthews, don't try to speak. I'm sure there is a lot you want to say, but it will be impossible as long as you are intubated. Please focus on resting, as that is what your body needs most right now. We will get you anything you need and when your body is able to, we will disconnect these machines and put you into a variety of therapies that will help your brain and your body to rebuild and heal. Do you understand?"

John continued to try to talk for a moment but resigned himself to simply nodding in agreement.

"Good," Dr. Jones said, and after he said it, he walked out of the room with Maria.

John was left alone in the room. He thought of all he just heard and it was all very overwhelming. Therefore, he closed his eyes and tried to sleep. All he could hear was the rhythmic breathing of the ventilator and the beeping of the machines measuring his heart and brain waves.

During the next week, John was sedated much of the time. His wife came in and saw him and sat by his bed. She read to him and talked to him in a soft and sweet voice. But John mostly just slept, spending most of his time in unconsciousness, searching for Sophia and Amoena Vieta. He kept writing on a notepad to Kristen that he has "so much to tell her."

At the end of the next week, Dr. Jones walked into John's room. John was exhausted and was nodding off. Kristen was sitting next to the bed. Dr. Jones cleared his throat and said, "John, I think your body is ready to come off some of these very uncomfortable machines. I'm going to take you off the ventilator today and the rest of the machines on Monday. I'd like to immediately put you into a physical therapy regimen to help your body retrain itself to function. Do you have any objections or questions about this?"

John shook his head. Kristen shook her head as well.

John was taken off the ventilator that day. His voice was hoarse and inaudible. Throughout the weekend, he practiced with Kristen, and his voice started as a whisper but built very slowly. After the next week, he was put in a physical therapy, cognitive therapy, and speech therapy regime. There were casts on his arm and legs, and there was not a great deal that he could perform. However, he did what he could and did so ardently and optimistically as he tried to accept his new fate in life.

By the end of the next week, his voice had returned. He was given a lot more freedom and was not confined to the hospital room entirely, although that is where he spent most of his time. Kristen came in the evenings after her job ended and the couple ate dinner together. The administrators at the hospital frequently talked to Kristen about their insurance and the mounting bill for John's considerable care. This stressed Kristen, but she tried not to focus on it. She tried to stay present with John.

One Tuesday evening, John was feeling well enough to talk to Kristen. He had been trying to do so ever since he had opened his eyes but could not. The two were in his hospital room while he lay in his bed. There was no more beeping and no more whirring of the machines. He had a tray in front of him of spaghetti and a side of vegetables. John reveled in eating the spaghetti and audibly enjoyed it. Kristen sat in a chair next to his bed and ate a salad. Her crunching was audible as John ate the spaghetti.

"It's really not bad hospital food," Kristen said to her husband. "I'm actually very surprised. Do you know the woman who crashed into you is here, too? She's a few rooms down. She's in rough shape but her girlfriend told me they think she'll be okay. From what the newspaper says, there weren't any fatalities from the accident. However, I do think the woman who hit you has a long road to recovery."

She said this to John but he did not seem to hear her. He was chewing a mouthful of spaghetti that he carefully twirled into a bunch on his spoon.

"John, what's going on with you? You're always staring into space since you came out of the coma. Do you want me to get Dr. Jones?"

John came out of his daydream. "No honey, there's no need. I'm very sorry about the woman and hope she is okay. But I was thinking about something I experienced that is more wonderful than anything I've ever experienced in my life." John lifted his plate of spaghetti from his lap and gently put it in Kristen's hands for her to put it on the table. "I'm so happy my voice is back so I can finally tell you. You see..."

For the next three hours and into the evening, John described everything about Amoena Vieta to his wife. He described what he saw and what heard and how he felt. He described all these things with a passion and fervor that animated his eyes and mouth and made him look much healthier. Kristen watched as he came alive and she also became pulled into the story of the Amoenians. John talked about what he saw and how it affected him. When John finished, he looked up at his wife and said,

"So don't you see?" he asked Kristen with quivering expectation in his voice. "I think that Sophia was saying that we – you and me and all of us," John said as his arm made a sweeping motion toward the window of the hospital, "*we* have to make it happen. I think she was saying that we have to start the change and constantly work to make society better. *We* do." John paused and took a sip of water. "So, what do you think, Kristen?"

John waited for a few moments and received no response from his wife. "Kristen, are you alright?" John asked before reaching his right hand out and placing it on top of hers.

Kristen blinked hard two times at John's warm touch. She looked like a shaman returning from a trance. Her arms rested on her lap.

"Yeah, sure, I'm fine, John," she said after clearing her throat. "I was just really thinking about some of the things Sophia told you, that's all." Kristen lifted her coffee and took a sip. She sat in the chair next to his bed and looked lost in thought.

"Well, what do you think of it?"

"I'm glad you told me, John. It was... interesting," she said before her lips pursed together, and she looked down at the table pensively. "Don't get me wrong, John, I think some of the things Sophia told you about could really work – and work well. I think some of them could really improve things here, you know? There are facets of the political setup of Amoena Vieta and Democratism, facets of the media and the tax system, and those of the legal system all appeal to me. In fact, I think *aspects* of everything that she described sound reasonable, pragmatic, and good. For instance, the use of computers," she said before tapping the laptop in front of her twice, "as the conduit of democracy does make a lot of sense."

"But other facets, the other aspects of the society – like the whole language thing, and the idea that the whole world lives without forming countries as if they were in one large Pangaea," she said before breaking into soft laughter, "those things just seem ridiculous to me, John."

"I know, Kristen," John interjected immediately. "But as you said, most of the systems in Amoenian society were feasible, and many of the systems were actually preferable to me. It's not like you have to embrace all of them – it's not an all-or-nothing deal. Forget about the language thing if you don't like it. But don't dismiss all of it based on a few things."

"Yeah, I see what you mean. And many of the social systems were preferable to me, too. I guess you're right."

"I'm thrilled you agree," John said with a child-like enthusiasm resonating in his voice. "I've been thinking about it as I was telling you the dream, and I think that the whole structure of Amoena Vieta really comes down to three basic ideals involved in the design of all the social systems. First, it has checks and balances to guide against the extremes of human nature. Second, it contained the idea that no one is an island, you know, that we are all part of each other and are responsible for each other and especially those who are struggling. Third, they believed that everyone's voice was important. That seems to be the basis upon which every societal institution is firmly rooted."

Kristen took another sip of coffee and casually looked past John and around the hospital room before responding, "Yeah, John, I can see all those being the basic themes. But it's kind of silly. I mean, the whole notion of a utopia – of a really pleasant place – it's nice and all, but it's impossible. Just look around at how bad it is here! And that's after thousands of years of trying! I don't even see the sense in discussing things like this. Life will always be full of strife no matter what humanity does to try to stop it."

John's eyes darkened as she finished. He put both elbows on the plastic railings on the sides of his bed and leaned forward toward Kristen. His voice became deeper and more serious than it had been in the three hours they spent together.

"But, Kristen! Don't you *see*? That was just what Sophia was *saying*! That was the most important point of all! That *we, as human* beings, can *never* stop trying to make the world a better place for each other and ourselves! Her whole point was that we must never cease trying to make our systems better. She was saying that we must unceasingly push ourselves toward our constructive, loving tendencies and never allow ourselves to fall too far into our destructive, hateful ones! All the systems she described were *theirs* – they don't necessarily have to be ours. We can just take what we like from them and create a society the way that *we – us – the human race* wants it to be through the compromise that is packaged with democracy. Through that unity we can create our own Amoena Vieta."

Kristen smiled, closed her eyes, and took a deep breath before speaking, "But. John –"

"No!" John interrupted vehemently as he reached toward Kristen and placed his index finger near Kristen's mouth. "*This* is the problem, Kristen. It's as clear as day. I know it's not an easy task! I know it's easy to give reason after reason why it can't be done or why it can't be done by you. And yes, it *will* be hard to make compromises and find midpoints in different viewpoints. But what's the alternative, Kristen? Apathy? Letting our systems and therefore our society continue to fall apart? Leaving the systems of injustice in place so that they may oppress the next generation?" John asked rhetorically. His eyebrows furrowed in solemn seriousness, and he looked deeply into Kristen's face. "Any society that stops trying to better itself is a dead society. If Sophia showed me anything, it's that we must never stop trying to improve the systems that serve as the gears in the machine of society. Apathy must be stopped!

We have to focus on real human progress, that is, the progress of the human spirit. That is the progress that will make our society a better place at no individual's or group's expense. We can't *ever* stop striving for our *collective* perfect place. We can't ever stop trying to form a society that satisfies all based on the common good of everyone. Don't you see, Kristen?"

The opposition that resided on Kristen's countenance moments before seemed to melt. "Well... yeah, I guess you're right there. We don't have much choice but to keep trying. But I don't see how it's on our shoulders, especially. I mean, we all have stock in the betterment of society. Let the others worry about it."

"It's not only our responsibility!" John said vehemently. "And it's not everyone else's, either. It's *all* of our responsibilities to create our own Amoena Vieta. That's the whole idea of a democracy – the responsibility is spread across the entire citizenry. The only way it can work as it should work is if everyone takes part in it. That's why there's mandatory voting in Amoena Vieta.

"We just need to be the catalyst that reminds everyone. *We, the people*, have the power *and* responsibility to make things better. Every one of us shares that responsibility. Besides, what choice do we have? The alternative is decadence and entropy – the death of civilized society and reverting back to the law of the survival of the fittest. The cycle of history and oppression will only begin anew unless we all come together and form our own Amoena Vieta. All we must do is get the people to agree that the *systems* we have set up in society need to be changed. If Sophia showed me anything, it's that people aren't the problem. It's the institutions we made. A few people, out of their own ignorance or greed, inevitably make the systems in such a way as to benefit them or a small group of people," John said before stopping and breathing heavily.

"Okay. What is this 'catalyst,' then? How can we possibly get all that started?"

"I'm not sure, Kristen. But based on all that Sophia just showed me – I'd say it's what's sitting right in front of us," John said as he motioned to the laptop that she had in a black bag next to her chair.

Kristen looked down, and her face blossomed into a smile. "Right... *computers... the internet* – they were the wheels of their democracy. Sophia said that many times!" Kristen said with mounting enthusiasm slipping into the tone of her voice.

John grinned and scratched the stubble on his face so hard that it sounded like sandpaper scratching on coarse oak. "Oh, thank God you understand, Kristen. Then... does that mean," he said bashfully, "does that mean you'll help?"

"Help what?"

"Help to try."

"How?"

John answered promptly, "Well, I've been taking lessons on the computer from my little brother on how to make webpages. I figure that webpages can be one conduit to the public in our attempt to get people interested and organized. I also have a buddy who works for the newspaper, so that'll be a help, too," John spoke more quickly and excitedly with each sentence, "When I get out of here and am back on my feet, I am going to create a blog link from the webpage so that people in the community can talk about the issues together. I will contact a buddy of mine in Wilkes-Barre, and I think he'll spread the word about our webpage there. I've already written an editorial in the paper this morning making an argument that everyone should have a computer and internet access as a right nowadays because of their growing importance in society. It may not be much, Kristen – but it's a start."

Kristen lifted her eyebrows and reached for her purse that was resting on the side of her chair opposite the laptop to get some gum. "I think Sophia," she paused, "I think *you* really have something here, John. I can feel your excitement, and I share it, too. We can start small – just like you're saying, and watch it grow like wildfire – on the internet and in town meetings, little by little, until every community in the country is revitalizing democracy by discussing meaningful change again. I have a friend who is a web developer and I can contact her to help us design the webpage along with your friend. She knows ways to advertise it online, too."

As Kristen spoke, her eyes drifted upward as if she were already seeing the multitude of people in meetings and behind keyboards all across the country discussing the ways in which they could ameliorate society. "You've got me so excited I want to get started today! When you're feeling better, we can work on it every weekend. We can use Sophia's ideas as a starting point for the discussion, and every week we can post and discuss a new issue... I really think this could work! I can almost see it, John!" Kristen said, still gazing into the air above John.

John and Kristen continued talking into the night. They discussed different ways they could utilize their resources to create a world like the one John saw. They talked about creating a world away from the systemic problems that limited their own freedom. They laughed and planned and talked in a way wherein the stifling systems of society suddenly seemed surmountable. The dream of Amoena Vieta began its ascent from John's unconscious into reality.

ACKNOWLEDGEMENTS

Thank you to my wonderful Mother, who showed me what utopia really means.

Thank you to the Black Spring Press Group for allowing a platform and voice for new ideas.